The Only Sound
in the Night Was
Raleigh's Ragged Breathing . . .

"Oh, sweet Jesus, Mara, you know I want you," he whispered.

"Then show me what to do. Make love to me, please," Mara said.

With Mara still on his lap, he bent over to spread the plaid blanket on the ground; then he lifted her onto it and slid down beside her.

"Lie on your side, facing me," he whispered.

Mara turned round. With her fingers, she lightly outlined his face.

He kissed her so thoroughly she felt warm all over, despite the chill wind blowing through their arbor against her unprotected back. But when Roy's arms went around her, he felt the wind, and he made her switch positions with him so that the rock slab sheltered her on one side, his body on the other. He unbuttoned her jacket, and his fingers began to move all over her with an instinctive, soft sensitivity . . .

Dear Reader,

We, the editors of Tapestry Romances, are committed to bringing you two outstanding original romantic historical novels each and every month.

From Kentucky in the 1850s to the court of Louis XIII, from the deck of a pirate ship within sight of Gibraltar to a mining camp high in the Sierra Nevadas, our heroines experience life and love, romance and adventure.

Our aim is to give you the kind of historical romances that you want to read. We would enjoy hearing your thoughts about this book and all future Tapestry Romances. Please write to us at the address below.

The Editors
Tapestry Romances
POCKET BOOKS
1230 Avenue of the Americas
Box TAP
New York, N.Y. 10020

Loving Longest

Jacqueline Marten

A TAPESTRY BOOK

PUBLISHED BY POCKET BOOKS NEW YORK

Books by Jacqueline Marten

English Rose
Irish Rose
French Rose
Loving Longest
An Unforgotten Love

Published by TAPESTRY BOOKS

This novel is a work of historical fiction. Names, characters, places
and incidents relating to non-historical figures are either the product
of the author's imagination or are used fictitiously. Any resemblance
of such non-historical incidents, places or figures to actual events or
locales or persons, living or dead, is entirely coincidental.

An *Original* publication of TAPESTRY BOOKS

A Tapestry Book published by
POCKET BOOKS, a division of Simon & Schuster, Inc.
1230 Avenue of the Americas, New York, N.Y. 10020

ISBN: 0-671-54608-2

First Tapestry Books printing January, 1986

10 9 8 7 6 5 4 3 2 1

POCKET and colophon are registered trademarks
of Simon & Schuster, Inc.

TAPESTRY is a registered trademark of Simon & Schuster, Inc.

Printed in the U.S.A.

For
Laure Horowitz
and
Barbara McWilliams
for themselves, of course,
and because they are Nita's daughters

Acknowledgment

To Linda Marrow, Editor, Friend,
and Favorite Companion
for the Logger's Breakfast.

All the privilege I claim for my own sex (it is not a very enviable one: you need not covet it), is that of loving longest, when existence or when hope is gone!

Anne Elliot in *Persuasion*
by Jane Austen

Chapter One

IN THE SPRING OF 1789, AT ABOUT THE TIME his monarch, George III, was recovering from his latest fit of madness, Cuthbert Rydale of Rydale Park near Carlisle in Cumbria County, England, arrived in Cairo with his Arab mistress, Haidee, and their baby son. Some three years and two additional sons later, after an eight-year sojourn in the Orient and the Holy Lands, Cuthbert returned to his native shores, landing at Plymouth.

Having supervised the unloading and shipping of some three dozen crates packed with purchased and purloined treasures from his travels, Cuthbert made all haste north in order to reach Rydale Park in time to attend his father's deathbed.

Sir Oliver, much gratified by this mark of filial respect from an only son, unseen for all eight years of his touring and unheard of for two, roused himself from a stupor—half induced by approaching death and half the result of an excellent bottle of port served with his evening meal—to offer his heir a final blessing as well as a few words of parting paternal admonition.

"Only son," he wheezed, then cackled a brief correction. "Only legitimate son. Rydales down to a pack of damn females—except you. Marry . . . fruitful . . . multiply."

Before he left Cairo, Cuthbert had handsomely dowered Haidee and arranged the future of their three sons. He therefore had no hesitation in offering a deathbed promise. "Your descendants shall people all Cumbria."

Greatly heartened by this arrogant assurance, Sir Oliver inhaled an excessive pinch of snuff and sneezed half a dozen times so vigorously, it put too much stress on his failing heart. On the sixth and last sneeze, his eyes opened wide in surprise and he was dead before his head fell back against the pillows.

Cuthbert, now *Sir* Cuthbert and the seventh Baron Rydale of Rydale Park, ordered deep mourning for himself and all his servants and commenced to make elaborate preparations for the funeral.

The Rydale connections scattered over England were bidden to attend the feasting that followed the late Sir Oliver's obsequies; the neighboring gentry from Carlisle, Ambleside, Egremont, Keswick, Kendal, Penrith, and even the Lake District were invited to partake of the funeral-baked meats and pies.

Sir Cuthbert's purpose in giving his father such a large and elegant send-off was twofold: to entomb his sire with proper pomp and propriety and then to look the field over and select the group of young women from whom, when his year of mourning was over, he could make his final choice of the one he would take to wife to mother his sons.

The funeral was over, most of the guests departed, and Sir Cuthbert had reached a decision. He would marry Lady Mary Anne Wordsworth, youngest of the five spinster daughters of the impoverished Earl of Kendal.

The Kendals were one of the first families in the county, and in past times could have looked much higher than a simple baron for one of their daughters. Gambling, drinking, dissolute living, and bad estate management, however, had brought their fortunes low and reduced their expectations. The Rydale monies, Sir Cuthbert felt sure, were more than a match now for Kendal blood; and Lady Mary Anne, in addition to her birth and breeding, looked a delectable morsel for bedding.

He had no idea that in choosing her, he was suffering a reaction to the lush, dark charms of his Arab mistress (and her equally dark-haired, olive-skinned, round-hipped, large-rumped maid when Haidee had been too pregnant).

Unknowingly, Lady Mary represented England to him . . . and pristine English beauty. She was sweetly shy and pinkly pretty with eyes of blue, ringlets of gold, smooth fair skin, and a pouting rosebud mouth. She was a tiny, fairylike creature, slim and straight and short enough to make Cuthbert feel tall.

She was barely out of the schoolroom, seventeen to his thirty, an age difference he approved of. It would make her docile and pliable, not setting her judgment up against his. He could mold her into what he willed.

Within a fortnight of making his choice, Sir Cuthbert, still garbed in the funereal black he would wear for another eleven months, paid a call on Lord Wordsworth, Earl of Kendal.

The two sat in his lordship's shabby library, where a superlative wine and stale biscuits were served to them by a maid in a soiled apron. Sir Cuthbert would have discharged her immediately; his lordship was evidently not so nice in his notions.

A few courtesies about the weather and their mutual health having been exchanged, Sir Cuthbert came straight to the point of his visit.

"I intend to observe the year of strict

4

mourning," he observed, and Lord Wordsworth bowed in acknowledgment. "After which," he went on, "I propose to marry."

Lord Wordsworth looked up, his face bright and interested.

"Your father's dearest wish, Sir Cuthbert," he commented piously.

Sir Cuthbert dried his lips delicately with a small serving cloth. "Naturally, no formal announcement can be made yet."

"Naturally."

"Still, there is no reason why the lady's father and I could not come to an agreement long before the year is up."

"No reason at all," echoed Lord Wordsworth, with an involuntary glance at the desk drawer where he had concealed a sheaf of unpaid bills when Sir Cuthbert was announced.

"I will be direct, my lord. I would be pleased to wed your daughter, the Lady Mary Anne."

"Lady M-Mary," faltered the father. "I would have thought. . . . Cecily and Sarah are nearer in age to you; you might deal better with one of them."

Sir Cuthbert smiled indulgently. Lady Cecily was eight and twenty, well past marriageable age; while Lady Sarah was a long Meg of a girl, topping him by some two inches. He needed no wife with *that* advantage.

He shook his head, still smiling.

"Emily?" offered Lord Wordsworth. "Margaret?"

Lady Emily was dark, big-nosed, and homely; Lady Margaret was pockmarked.

Sir Cuthbert frowned his displeasure. "I am offering for the Lady Mary Anne." He paused delicately. "No other."

The Earl of Kendal, alarmed that he might have let this plump fish swim off his hook, said overheartily, "She is yours then, sir. That is"—he paused to pluck a scrap of lint off his brocade waistcoat—"if we can come to a satisfactory agreement."

"If you will give me the name and direction of your attorney, I will have my own contact him. To make the Lady Mary Anne mine," he added, filling the heart of his host with gladness, "I am prepared, my lord, to be generous."

Within six weeks settlements had been agreed on and contracts drawn up—even the wedding date set for the second week in June of 1793, following a betrothal period of two months.

All that remained was to inform the bride, and this need not be done for some time.

"She might not be able to keep her good fortune to herself," said Lord Wordsworth, uncomfortably aware that in frank family discussions, Sir Cuthbert had not figured overfavorably in Lady Mary Anne's conversation, "and I would by no means wish to show disrespect to your father's memory."

"You are in the right of it," the seventh Baron Rydale agreed amiably, and went home to Rydale Park, prepared to wait for his chosen bride in the greatest comfort.

He was a man of little emotion but large sexual appetite. Emma, the new parlor maid, had lately caught his eye and laughingly fended off his advances.

She was a healthy country girl with rosy cheeks, merry brown eyes, and thick, curly russet hair. Not only her looks and vitality attracted Sir Cuthbert; he was intrigued that a parlor maid remained unawed by the distinction of a baron's attentions and the generosity of his bribes.

In the end her very health and vitality betrayed Emma. She was ripe and ready for a man's arms, and the single-mindedness of Sir Cuthbert in pursuit combined with his vigor as a lover were too much for her.

On the day in his library that he bestowed a gold locket on her, she allowed as how he might have a few kisses. The kisses proved so enjoyable to both that soon his hands were inside her bodice, then beneath her skirt and sliding up her legs.

As he clasped her bottom and rubbed against her, Sir Cuthbert thought of telling her to creep up the back stairs to his room, then changed his mind, judging it best he not give her time to cool down. With his hands once again under her petticoats, he lowered her to the precious Persian carpet that had been uncrated only the week before.

Emma's symbol of virginity was quickly dispatched and proved no bar to their pleasure. As soon as Cuthbert recovered from his climax, he stood up, putting his clothes to rights. Emma lay curled on the carpet, looking like a clothed Botticelli angel.

"You had best get up, my dear," Sir Cuthbert told her. "Handley may come in at any moment with my wine."

"Coo!" Emma sprang to her feet. "My petticoats aren't half messed up."

"Better your petticoats than my carpet." As he spoke his hand caressed the curve where her rounded hip disappeared into a deliciously taut buttock. "Buy yourself some petticoats in town on your next half day . . . of the finest lawn . . . I'll provide the coin. And meet me in my bedroom in say half an hour's time."

"Half an hour," agreed Emma, eyeing him as hungrily as he was eyeing her.

Their liaison continued for quite awhile and ended about four months before Sir Cuthbert's formal betrothal to Lady Mary Anne Wordsworth would have brought it to a natural conclusion.

Lying in his arms in his bedroom one night, Emma said matter-of-factly, "I'm going to have a baby, sir."

Sir Cuthbert sat up. "The devil you are!"

Then he looked down at her lovely naked form. "You do look a bit full-bellied," he admitted, rather more pleased than not. After all, he had provided for his bastards before. It was a matter of proper planning and money wisely spent; and after a whole seven months with him, it would have been more extraordinary if Emma had *not* been pregnant.

"How far along are you?" he asked her.

"Three months, I would reckon, perhaps a week or two the other way."

Sir Cuthbert lay back, with one arm under her and one thrown across her full belly.

"Emma, my girl," he said, "I think it's time you got yourself a husband."

They both knew he did not mean himself.

"Aye," said Emma placidly, pleasantly. "I think that would be best."

"Do you have any candidates at home in Yorkshire?"

"Sir?"

"Is there anyone from your home village you've a mind to?"

"No, sir."

"Shall I find you someone?"

"No, sir. I know who I want—a lad from hereabouts—if he'll have me."

"Indeed?" said Sir Cuthbert Rydale, not best pleased.

"Aye," said Emma, unruffled. "You'll perhaps know Mr. Jonas Benton, the gentleman

9

farmer who owns Treeways Farm, north-ways of the river Eden, halfway from Carlisle to the Scots border."

"I've met him," said Sir Cuthbert, his frown easing. "He's a mid-aged widower without children."

His own bride would be eighteen to his thirty-one; he was pleased at the notion of Emma and his child going to a mid-aged widower!

"Mr. Benton has a helper named Angus MacTavish, a Scotsman hired out to him these last ten years. He's the one."

"How old?"

"Twenty-four or five, I think, Sir Cuthbert; I don't know for sure."

"Not such a lad then. And how do you come to know him?"

"We've met at parties and dances and once at the fair and just last week at the horse auction."

"And you like him?"

"Aye, sir."

"And he likes you?"

"Being a Scot, he's never said so, but I have the sense he does, sir."

His hand tightened around her wrist.

"Have you had aught to do with Mac-Tavish, Emma? I'm willing to provide for my own bastards . . . but not one I might be sharing with another man. I'll have the truth out of you, my girl."

Emma lay looking up at him, her eyes wide but unafraid.

"I'm not a loose girl for all I gave myself to you, Sir Cuthbert. I didn't lie with you for your gifts and I don't lie with but one man at a time, which makes you the only man I've ever lain with. It could only be your child growing inside me, and it's possible Angus MacTavish may not want me when I tell him."

"He'll want you," said Sir Cuthbert cynically. "Haven't I heard that Benton is seeking a partner with money for Treeways?"

"Aye, and Angus has none. The better part of his wages go to support his parents in Scotland; his father's an invalid."

"The day this Angus weds you he'll have the money for his partnership with Mr. Benton; he'll own half of Treeways Farm. I'll put money with my attorney to educate a boy or dower a girl . . . so he'll have no responsibility there. Do you want me to approach him for you?"

"I think I had better do it myself, sir. It's a delicate matter."

Sir Cuthbert snorted disbelievingly. To his mind, there wasn't a lowborn Englishman alive—let alone a Scot—who would turn down a partnership in a prosperous farm out of finicking reluctance to father another man's bastard!

Chapter Two

EMMA WAS GIVEN THE NEXT DAY OFF AS WELL as the loan of the donkey cart. Ostensibly she was going to Carlisle on an errand for the housekeeper, but as soon as she was out of sight of Rydale, she changed direction and headed for Treeways Farm.

A few moments after she came onto the Benton property, she had the good fortune to find Angus MacTavish alone in the south field. She recognized him immediately but slowed down and gave him the chance to see and hail her first. Then she brought her donkey to a full stop and waited.

Angus came bounding over the fence and onto the road, looking—in his corduroy breeches, open waistcoat, and work shirt—exactly what he was, a sturdy farmer.

He might lack the elegant strength and lean, aristocratic features of Sir Cuthbert, but the greenish eyes of the farm lad had a twinkling good humor entirely lacking in the baron. The strength of Sir Cuthbert's arms was limited to the bedroom. The strength of Angus' arms, Emma thought with a pang of regret, would be there for his woman forever.

"What are you doing here, lass?" exclaimed Angus in delight.

Emma smiled back at him. "Delivering a note to Mr. Benton from my master." Then she looked solemnly at the hands folded over the reins in her lap. "Though I did hope to see you to say good-bye."

"Good-bye," repeated Angus. Then, as though tasting the words on his tongue, he said again, "Good-bye. Where are you going, girl—and why? Have you been dismissed from Rydale?"

"Nay, not that, but I have to go from there."

"*Have* to?"

"Aye."

"Am I to know the reason?" he asked slowly.

"I have to go home to my own folk before I begin to show," she blurted out. "I'm with child."

"You canna wed the father?"

"*He* can't wed *me*," she admitted honestly. "Nor do I want him."

Up till then the unblinking green eyes had contained no trace of bitterness or blame.

Suddenly they were darkly stormy. She shivered at the coldness in his voice. "If you don't want him, why are you with child by him?"

Emma looked down again. "It was . . . oh, I don't know . . . exciting, I expect, to be pursued and wooed by someone so above me. I was like a little one playing with fire and thinking she's not about to be burned. I kept telling myself, 'It's your game, Emma, you can stop any time you want to' . . . but it really wasn't . . . he knew the moves better than I did."

"It's your master you're talking about, isn't it . . . Sir Cuthbert Rydale, the dirty lecherous swine?"

"Nay." Emma shook her head. "I can't put the blame more on him than on myself. I knew what I was doing. He didn't take me unwilling."

"Tell me, Emma, when you first went to him, was it—was it after that night we danced together at Sawyer's Farm or the afternoon we spent at the fair?"

She shook her head. "It started last winter. 'Twas after the night we danced I first felt regret, and all through our Fair Day, whenever I thought of it, I was pierced by shame. I wanted to stop then, but I didn't know where to go without leaving here . . . leaving you . . . and then I found out about the child."

She ventured a quick look up at him from under her lashes. The green eyes were thoughtful, his face sadly serious, and his mouth was a firm straight line.

"I'd best take my note to the house," said Emma, picking up the reins.

"I'll wed with you, Emma," said Angus, "if you'll have *me*."

She had come there intending to wring that very proposal out of him. Now that she had, dull red color filled her cheeks. She found herself inquiring urgently, "Why?"

The green eyes were unblinking, unwavering. "Well do you know why."

"Nay," said Emma shrilly. " 'Tis not possible." She gave the reins a fierce tug. "I have to go."

"Stay a moment." He put his hand on the side of the cart, but Emma only shook her head and reached down for the whip to slap it across the donkey's flanks.

As she tried to move forward, Angus struggled to clamber over the side of the cart. She used her elbow to try to shove him backward, but after a few minutes his greater strength prevailed. She was the one shoved aside as Angus heaved himself onto the seat beside her and seized the reins.

"Now what was all that foolishness?" he asked sternly. "If this animal had the brain of a flea and had heeded your whip, you could have been hurt. I'm of a mind to take my hand to you." Saying which, he folded her into his arms instead. "You're *going* to marry me, my lass," he told her.

"It was another game I played," Emma confessed wretchedly. "I came here in hopes of getting you to ask me, just as you did."

The hint of a smile quivered on his lips. "Do you take me for a fool, my Emma? I knew well what you were after."

Emma's lips were parted, her brown eyes wide with shock. "Then why—"

"You were ashamed of the game, weren't you? You told me the truth?"

"Aye."

"Then that's good enough for me, lass, since I love you mightily. Just one thing more. A condition, you might say."

"Yes, Angus?"

"The day I wed with you both you and the bairn become mine. I'm not a man to share what's mine. D'you *ken* what I'm saying?"

"I'll be a true and faithful wife to you, Angus MacTavish, if wife I become, but I've a condition of me own. However he was got, the babe is innocent. I'll not have a child of mine growing up in the shadow of a sin that was not his but his mother's. If you can't accept him with a full heart as your own, if you'll fear to look at him for the anger you'll feel for how he was begotten—or for that matter at *me*—then it's best that we part now."

Angus sat beside her deep in thought, and Emma's heart was wrenched with pain that she had lost him by asking too much.

"How far along are you?" he inquired presently.

"Close on three months."

"In that case, it's better we not wait to post the banns. Another three weeks of waiting would be foolish. What's to prevent our going over the border to Gretna Green this very day? We could be husband and wife by nightfall and no need for you ever to go back to Rydale. My hut isn't much—just the one room—but I'm sure as a married man, Mr. Benton would give me something better soon. He's a good man."

Emma opened her mouth, then closed it.

"Well?" Angus urged.

"It's s-so quick."

"The quicker the better, it would seem to me," said Angus dryly, with a meaning look at her waistline.

Emma blushed. "My clothes are all at the Park," she said in a low voice.

"I'll fetch them for you tomorrow. I don't want you ever again at Rydale," he said again.

On their way to the farmhouse to deliver Sir Cuthbert's note to Mr. Benton and acquaint him with his hired man's intent to go into Scotland to take a wife, Angus asked her, "Will you mind being married over the anvil, lass?"

"I'll take you any which way I can get you, Angus MacTavish."

Angus wrenched at the reins and pulled the poor puzzled donkey to a halt again so he could seize her in his arms and shower kisses onto her face. He continued to do the same at intervals all during their trip to the border till Emma said laughingly, even as she returned his kisses, "At the pace you're going, we'll not be wed today."

"Oh yes, we will," Angus promised; and wed they were, by the first blacksmith they encountered a few yards from where they crossed the border, using as witnesses two Scotsmen waiting to have their horses shod.

When they returned to Treeways, a roaring fire had been lit and a fine wedding supper set out in the small hut where Angus lived. A note from Mr. Benton told Angus that his former hired man was now his partner in the farm and would move into Treeways Cottage next month when his farm manager retired.

Supper grew cold while the husband and wife had the first quarrel of their marriage. It raged on for half an hour, with voices high and tempers hot on both sides.

"You think you're being bribed to father Sir Cuthbert Rydale's bastard child," Emma said finally, "and your Scots pride is affronted."

"You're right it's affronted, and you're right, that's what I think," Angus unclenched his teeth to retort.

"Well, it's no such thing!" flared Emma. "And the devil with your Scots pride. Bad enough I feel that I come to you with this unwelcome gift in my belly. Now you're refusing to accept my dower money."

"Your *dower* money! A partnership in a farm like Treeways a parlor maid's dower!" Angus gasped. "Woman, you're daft!"

"I may be daft, but my English pride is no less than yours. If you're not willing to have my dowry, then you can't have me."

"I've already got you, Emma MacTavish."

"Oh no, you haven't, Angus MacTavish. We may have said the words, and they may have been put on paper. You can even take me, willing or not, to your bed, but if I choose to withhold myself from you, then you'll never have me, man, not if we have a dozen children more and live together for the next twoscore years."

Angus pounded his fists on the table in exasperation, setting the plates to jingling. "You contrary English lass!"

"You thick-headed Scot!"

"Mule!"

"Donkey!"

"Your backside needs warming."

"Your brain needs airing."

He raised his hand, and she lifted a pewter mug just as threateningly. They glared at each other for a moment and then suddenly, simultaneously, both burst out laughing and fell into each other's arms, still choked with laughter as they kissed.

When they finally broke apart, "I'm

starved," Emma said, prepared to sit down at the table.

"So am I." Angus swung her up into his arms and carried her across the room to the narrow bed in the corner.

Sometime later he gasped out hoarsely, "That was dower enough for me, my love, my lass."

"But you'll take the rest that comes with me, won't you, my own true love?" Emma coaxed, while one hand caressed his chest and the other fondled him in an even more privileged and private way.

"Dear God," Angus muttered, "it's little wonder Adam was so quick to eat the apple."

"Will you eat of the fruit, too, Angus Mac-Tavish?"

"So long as you go with it, lassie."

"I do, my mannie, I do, indeed."

Chapter Three

Dᴜʀɪɴɢ ᴛʜᴇ ᴄᴏᴜʀsᴇ ᴏꜰ ʜɪs ᴡᴇᴅᴅɪɴɢ ʀᴇᴄᴇᴘ-
tion at Kendal Court, Sir Cuthbert learned
from Thomas Benton of Treeways, invited
with other minor neighborhood gentry, that
Emma MacTavish was the mother of a fine
stout boy.

Another son.

To the proud Sir Cuthbert, it seemed a
happy portent of things to come. He could
scarcely wait for the end of the marriage
festivities to take his bride home to bed.

Bless God it was only a three-hours carriage drive to Rydale, and bless his own
prudence for firmly declining Lady Wordsworth's proposal of a wedding trip.

"I have had enough traveling to suffice me
for the next dozen years, my lady," he had
told her most decidedly. "Mary will have to
be satisfied with a diamond set instead."

Lady Mary had been more than satisfied at

the time. Diamonds were what every woman wanted—weren't her very own sisters all wild with envy? Besides, she tended to get woefully carriage-sick.

She began to change her mind as she waited for her husband in her elaborate, new-furnished bedchamber at Rydale, wearing the long, loose silken gown and robe prudently chosen by her mother for ease of removal. Her mama's admonitions about "duty" and "endurance" sounded warningly in her ears. The mysterious hints about "men being different" and "learning to cope with the beast in their natures" were causing the little bride's knees to buckle in fright.

That was what Sir Cuthbert saw when he came to claim her, a childlike figure who barely filled out the seductive gown. She was trembling visibly; her eyes were round and bright with fear. As well as get some sons upon her, it would be enjoyable, he thought, to bring such childish frightened innocence to passion.

For all his experience, and though he could certainly claim having had more virgins than just Emma, Sir Cuthbert had dealt with only passionate women. Lady Mary was no more a woman at eighteen than she had been at eight or would be at eight and twenty. Lady Mary was and always would be a child.

A passionless husband might have succeeded with her but never Sir Cuthbert Ry-

dale. His kisses did not soothe, they suffo-
cated her. His caresses did not calm, they
terrified. Like a sleepwalker, she allowed
him to lead her to the bed, lift up her night
rail, and arrange her limbs.

"No, no," she moaned feebly when he announced with satisfaction that he had
reached her virgin's shield.

Accustomed to moans that indicated pleasure and no's that really meant yes, Sir Cuthbert proceeded straightaway to the business
at hand.

It was far from as easy as it had been with
Emma. Impeded by the shrinking reluctance
of his bride, who whimpered and wept
throughout, Sir Cuthbert strove mightily for
twenty minutes. As her bridegroom's objec-
tive was finally achieved, Lady Mary uttered
a piercing scream. Even Sir Cuthbert could
not mistake it for a scream of pleasure.

He patted her shoulder consolingly. "Rest
a little," he said. "Now that you are not
virgin, there will be no hurt the next time."

"N-next t-time," faltered poor Lady Mary
Anne Rydale. "You mean—again—tonight?"

Sir Cuthbert stroked the flat little stomach
of his bride and pinched one of her bony hips.
"Of course, tonight," he assured her jovially.
"We want this"—he slapped her belly lightly
again—"bursting with our son soon, do we
not?"

Tears having failed, Lady Mary tried her
best to swoon. Her husband put burnt feath-

ers under her nose; he comforted and consoled her. Then, as soon as she was calm again, he proceeded to exercise the rights that her mama had said she must learn to endure.

Lady Mary learned quickly. Her husband might be carelessly generous about her allowance and shrug off her inability to manage a household. He never took her to task for her limited conversation or her lamentable lack as a hostess. But about one thing he was adamant—her bedroom duties.

Until he got her with child, she must continue to suffer the length and strength of his almost nightly attentions.

Lady Mary, though entirely without maternal yearnings, began to pray most heartily to be pregnant.

Almost at once her prayers were answered and her husband informed. The happy news having been confirmed by an eminent physician summoned from Harrowgate in Yorkshire, Sir Cuthbert paid a rare afternoon visit to his bride's bedroom.

He kissed her hand, as he had in the days of their courtship, and then, almost paternally, her cheek.

"You have done well, my dear. I am pleased."

"Th-thank you, Sir Cuthbert."

"I am going to Carlisle to that shop on Castle Street to purchase the ruby pendant that I remember you took a fancy to."

"Oh, thank you, Sir Cuthbert."

"You must rest a good deal and take care of yourself. Don't worry your little head about household duties; Mrs. Nelson will manage it all. Your health must come first." He smiled kindly down on her. "Which is why I shall not come to you until after the boy is weaned, you take my meaning?"

Lady Mary "took" his meaning only too well. With unusual tact she restrained her impulse to cry out a third time, "Oh, thank you, Sir Cuthbert!"

"Whatever you say, my lord," she murmured submissively.

Her husband smiled, not misliking this elevation, patted her head paternally again, and ran down the broad steps to the hallway, whistling cheerfully.

With the ruby pendant tucked into his waistcoat pocket and a pile of fashion magazines, a Gothic novel, and a bag of sweetmeats underneath the racing sheet in his saddlebags, he rode to an inn on the other side of Carlisle.

Having provided generously for his wife, he now proposed to see to his own needs. He had noticed the innkeeper's young serving wench a few weeks before. A comely lass, dark-haired, dark-eyed, round and plump. Except for her white skin, she reminded him of Haidee.

Within a week the wench—Millie Sloan— was established in a four-room cottage neither too near nor too far from Rydale, with a middle-aged maid chosen for her by Sir Cuthbert as both helper and guardian of his rights.

The maid, Hannah, melted discreetly away when Sir Cuthbert came to visit . . . and Sir Cuthbert came often because he soon discovered that in Millie he had found the ideal mate. She possessed a sexual appetite as great as his own and an otherwise completely undemanding nature. She never asked for anything he did not choose to give; she never whined or complained. She was perfectly happy with him when he was there, but when he was gone seemed equally happy with her chickens and goats and vegetable garden, her knitting and sewing and the placid company of Hannah.

Millie possessed a wry, earthy sense of humor that appealed to Sir Cuthbert and a commonsense practical turn of mind he found surprisingly useful. It was an unexpected bonus to be able to discuss the management of his estates and get good advice from a serving wench out of an inn.

He would keep Millie, Cuthbert soon decided, even next year after the child was weaned and he had to return to his wife's bed. That, after all, would only be brief duty . . . to beget more heirs; *this* was for his own enjoyment.

His satisfaction with Millie combined with

his pleasure in having so soon fathered a legitimate son made Sir Cuthbert even kinder and more patient with his pretty, prattling, boring little bride, who blossomed under his affectionate care, his paternal ways.

"I think you had better get some rest, my dear," he would say gently when her tinkling voice began to grate on his nerves.

"Yes, sir."

Like an obedient little girl, Lady Mary would rise, dip a small curtsy, and retire to her room, where her maids—she had two now—would fuss over her, fix her possets, fetch her wine and sweet biscuits, comb out her hair, rub away her aches and pains with sweet oils, and endlessly discuss her gowns and her jewels, her hairstyles and her shoe roses.

For nearly three months Lady Mary's life was all honey and roses; no cross word was ever said to her, no responsibility given her. The minimal discomforts of her pregnancy were all made easier for her by an indulgent husband and eager servitors.

The serpent in her paradise struck suddenly and swiftly in the fifth month of her pregnancy.

During the early weeks of their marriage Sir Cuthbert had given her a sweet little white kitten, conditioning only that it be left to live in the stables. Lady Mary consented readily and for months made daily visits to Snowball in the stables until she became rather heavier with child and often lazy. Then she started coaxing her maids to smuggle Snowball into the house to visit her.

Just lately they had begun to object. Snowball was becoming heavier, too, more cat than kitten. It was growing difficult to carry him back and forth, and they did not wish to incur Sir Cuthbert's displeasure.

Lady Mary would look up at one or the other of them from the lounge where she half lay, half sat, golden curls cascading down her muslin-clad shoulders, a satin coverlet across her legs.

Her lips would quiver piteously. "I did *so* want to see Snowball, and I'm so *very* tired."

One of the little serving girls, who worked from dawn till long after their mistress was abed, would always succumb. "Very well, Lady Mary, but just this one time more."

Snowball would be fetched, and Lady Mary would throw a ball of yarn and play with him for perhaps twenty minutes. Sometimes Snowball would curl up beside her, his furry hindquarters nestling enjoyably against her belly. Occasionally the cat accepted, with uneasy tolerance, one of Lady Mary's convulsive embraces.

The accident occurred when the mistress forgot, as she hugged her cat, the two pins she had placed in her bodice to indicate the torn lace edging that Louise or Amy must sew.

With an angry yowl, Snowball pawed furiously with uncut claws at Lady Mary. She gave a startled scream and put up her arm to protect her face. The arm was scratched viciously; she tried to move backward out of harm's way and tripped over an embroidered footstool, falling heavily.

The child was the expected son, but it did not survive so premature a birth.

Of all those involved in his loss, his wife was the one Sir Cuthbert never forgave. Snowball disappeared, never to be seen again, and no one dared inquire his fate. The maids Amy and Louise were summoned to their master's study the next day, trembling in fear of being dismissed without a character. They were given the alternative of a sound thrashing.

With his own hands and his own riding whip, Sir Cuthbert administered the thrashing, then promptly forgot their share in depriving him of his heir.

He could not, unfortunately for his temper, beat his wife, pitiful sickly creature that she was and all his hopes of legitimate sons still bound up in her.

With great effort, he managed to be soothing and kind in her presence and, greatly to their mutual relief, stayed away from her as much as he was able.

The doctor had suggested six months' time before Sir Cuthbert return to his wife's bed, but pressed, admitted that yes, perhaps three would be enough. During those three months Sir Cuthbert was more often at Millie Sloan's cottage than he was at Rydale.

Chapter Four

TWELVE WEEKS TO THE DAY THAT SHE MIS-carried, Sir Cuthbert came through the two dressing rooms—his, then hers—and entered his wife's bedroom.

She knew what he was there for and did not dare object, but she was even more frightened than on her wedding night. Slowly, silently, she removed her dressing gown and night dress and lay flat on the bed.

Sir Cuthbert knew what he was there for too. He looked down at the vapid, waxen face he no longer found the least bit pretty, at the motionless, still childlike body. She nervously construed the low cry he gave as one of passion when it was no such thing.

For the first time in his life, Cuthbert was looking at naked female flesh without so much as a quiver in his loins. He felt nothing, nothing at all.

He flung off his robe and fell on his wife in

a spirit of cold determination. After ten ago-
nizing minutes he managed to arouse himself by imagining her to be Millie, lovely
Millie, plump, round, responsive Millie. Carried away by his fantasies about his mistress,
Cuthbert was finally able to couple enjoyably
with his own wife. That night. Almost every
night. For all the long months till Lady Mary
was once again pregnant.

From the moment the local midwife declared it to be so, Lady Mary scarcely moved
from her apartment, except for a daily walk
around the gardens on her husband's arm or
a rare visit to her parents. She was hedged
about with rules and restrictions, and so
were her maids. Sir Cuthbert summoned
Amy and Louise to his study to warn them
coldly there would be no second chance if
they dared disobey him.

Even when she walked down the stairs to
lunch or supper, if Sir Cuthbert was not there
to attend her, then the butler must go before
her and a footman behind.

After her fifth month a baby nurse was
moved into Lady Mary's dressing room to
constantly attend her. The nurse was a pleasant, sensible body who insisted her patient
get more fresh air and exercise—"for the
child's sake, Sir Cuthbert"—an appeal not
made in vain.

She also, secretly, without alarming the
master, cut down on the extraordinarily
large number of dainty glasses filled with

wine that Lady Mary was managing to down each day—particularly before a meeting with her husband.

The midwife and local doctor were sent for as soon as Lady Mary went into labor two weeks early. At the same time the butler dispatched a discreet message to Millie Sloan's cottage, where Sir Cuthbert and his mistress sprawled comfortably across the four-poster he had bought her when she announced that she was pregnant too.

Sir Cuthbert came galloping home, arriving at his gates at the same time as Dr. Greene.

"My deepest regrets, Sir Cuthbert," the doctor apologized obsequiously, "but your message reached me late. I was out at Treeways Farm seeing to Emma MacTavish when your coachman came to fetch me."

"Emma MacTavish?" Sir Cuthbert smiled reminiscently.

"She had another fine boy," the doctor said as Handley opened the front door.

The house was hushed, but halfway up the stairs, a baby's cry pierced the stillness. Both men took the rest of the steps at a bound.

Near the door to Lady Mary's bedroom stood the nurse and midwife and Amy and Louise, all bent over the wrapped bundle in Nurse's arms, all looking happy and excited.

By God, he had done it!

Sir Cuthbert strode forward, holding out his arms. "Give me my son."

The bundled baby was placed in his arms. He looked down at it for the only two seconds of such awed delight he would ever feel.

The rest of the women fell back uneasily, but the midwife—who did not serve in his household—spoke up with impudent good cheer. "You've got yourself a daughter this time, sir. If it's a son you're wanting, you will have to try again."

Sir Cuthbert looked down at the bundle he was holding, feeling the awe, the delight, all the pleasure drain away. Silently he handed his daughter over to the nurse.

"My wife?" he asked the midwife coldly.

"She be fine but mortal tired. Best not go in now . . . her be asleep."

Sir Cuthbert pushed past her and closed the door. He stood a moment with his back to it. He had three sons growing up in Egypt now, and he had given Emma MacTavish one of her two. Why then couldn't that whey-faced cold fish he was married to do anything right? He approached the bed.

Lady Mary wasn't asleep, just lying very quiet, very still, her face quite white, her eyes growing wary when she saw the look in his.

"She's . . . they tell me she's very healthy," she offered in a thin thready voice.

"I shall call her Mara," Sir Cuthbert answered harshly.

Lady Mary took heart. If he was thinking of naming the baby after *her*, he must not be quite so displeased with her as she had imagined.

"I would like her to be Mary," she acknowledged with a timid smile.

"Not Mary, Mara." He spelled it out for her. "From the Biblical admonition," he added brutally. "'*Call me Mara, the bitter . . . for the Almighty hath dealt very bitterly to me.*'"

Lady Mary closed her eyes. It was the only way she knew to shut him out. When she opened them again, he was gone. The nurse was back with her baby.

"It's time to suckle the little one, Lady Mary." Nurse smiled.

Lady Mary crossed her arms over her small breasts. "I don't want to. Let someone else go through that disgusting business. I'd have done it for a son to keep *him* away from me . . . but not for her. She should have been a boy. Take her away."

The baby wailed hungrily all night, unsoothed by sugared tits and drops of milk squeezed into her mouth from the finger of a glove.

In the morning after another vain appeal to Lady Mary, Nurse approached Sir Cuthbert at the breakfast table. "We need a wet nurse for the baby, sir."

"Why not my wife?"

"She hasn't enough milk, Sir Cuthbert," Nurse lied.

"I should have known." A peculiarly unpleasant smile crossed his face. "She can't do anything that other women do."

"She just had a baby," Nurse couldn't forbear pointing out.

"A girl." He clipped out the two words in a voice that dismissed any false notion of accomplishment. "Well, do what you can . . . get a wet nurse, if you must, or better still, put her out to one . . . it will be less bother."

"But who, sir?"

"Why ask me? Do I know every farm girl who's whelped recently? Send an inquiry to Dr. Greene. No, stay a moment . . ." A twisted smile returned to his face. "Try Emma MacTavish at Treeways Farm. She just had another son yesterday, and God knows she's healthy and common enough to be cow to a whole herd of calves. Send word that I'll pay whatever she wants."

"If her baby was born just yesterday, she can't come here, sir. Can someone take me and the babe to her?"

"Handley." Sir Cuthbert looked up at the butler, who was standing by, his face impassive.

"Yes, Sir Cuthbert?"

"Order the carriage to be ready in thirty minutes, when I am done with my breakfast." He turned back to Nurse. "I'll take you myself. Be ready in the driveway in a half-hour's time." He waved her off.

"And back he goes to his eating," she reported fiercely to Amy and Louise moments later as she wrapped the baby in a blanket, "stuffing his own face as slow and easy as you please, while this poor little mite is too weak with hunger to cry anymore. That's the gentry for you."

Despite her disdain she did not dare keep the gentry waiting but came down the steps ahead of the appointed time to find Sir Cuthbert just stepping into the back of his coach.

While Nurse scrambled up behind him, a footman held the baby. As soon as the wrapped bundle was handed up to her, the steps were put up, the door shut, and the carriage moved forward.

Sir Cuthbert turned his head a fraction of an inch for the briefest glance at the whimpering child.

"She sounds sickly."

"She's a fine healthy child," Nurse defended stoutly, "but she's half starved now."

"Humph."

It was the last word spoken during the hour's journey.

When the carriage came to a stop, Sir Cuthbert got down, leaving Coachman to help Nurse and the baby. He looked at Treeways Cottage, enclosed in its own neat garden and prettified with a veranda and French windows.

Many a young lady might have envied such a setting, let alone an unlettered parlor maid. Emma MacTavish had landed soft, all right, thanks to him.

Sir Cuthbert strode into the house without knocking, paused to glance at a pleasantly furnished if somewhat shabby little drawing room. He followed the sound of voices to the kitchen.

A gray-haired woman in snowy apron and cap stood at the stove, stirring the good-smelling stew in a huge iron pot. In a rocking chair near the fireplace, her little slippered feet set firmly on a hassock, sat Emma MacTavish, a baby suckling at one bare, shapely breast.

"Good morning, Sir Cuthbert," Emma said in a soft, clear voice. She sat serene and unembarrassed, making no effort to cover her breast. By God, but she was something! The pretty girl had become as handsome a woman as any in Cumbria. If having sons did this for a woman, he had double reason for wanting a dozen out of Mary.

"Mam," said Emma, "this is Sir Cuthbert from Rydale Park, where I used to work. Sir Cuthbert, this is my mother come from Yorkshire to be with me at the birth. And this"—she touched the small fuzzy-headed baby making the voraciously loud suckling sounds—"this is Donnie."

"Pleased to make your acquaintance, sir," said Emma's mother in a broad Yorkshire accent, bobbing a respectful curtsy.

Sir Cuthbert gave the woman a brief nodding acknowledgment. "You've an older son, I believe?" he said to Emma.

"Duggie," she said, eyeing him steadily, "short for Douglas. He'll be two next month. What can I do for you, Sir Cuthbert?"

"My wife had a daughter yesterday, and the child needs a wet nurse. When Greene told me that you'd had a second son, I thought you might be of help."

Emma frowned slightly, thinking of Angus, who might not be best pleased. She wasn't sure she liked the idea herself.

"Have you not milk enough?" Sir Cuthbert asked abruptly.

"Aye, that would not be the problem."

"I'll pay you whatever you consider it worth," he said with insolent disdain.

Emma drew herself up as haughtily as any lady-born. She was neither his parlor maid nor his mistress anymore but the wife of Angus MacTavish and the mother of *his* two sons. She was mistress of *this* kitchen and *this* house and had a parlor maid of her own!

"Money would not be the question either, Sir Cuthbert. I don't wish any if I do you this favor," she told him proudly. "But while we discuss it, I think you should have the child brought inside here. A newborn babe should not be out in the wind."

Sir Cuthbert turned sharply and left the room. He was not angered by her pride or her plain speaking. By God, but she was something, he said to himself again. If only Mary had a tenth of her spirit and vitality. At times like these he conveniently forgot he had chosen Mary for her birth and breeding, her milk-and-water manners, and her pale pink prettiness.

When he returned to the kitchen, Nurse, with the whimpering Mara in her arms, trailed after him. Emma's mother was putting the sleeping Donnie into a hand-carved cradle and Emma was still in the rocker, a large Shetland shawl wrapped snugly about her.

Emma could hear the continual soft complaints of Lady Mary's baby; she sounded like a mewling kitten.

"Let me see her."

Nurse handed the baby down to her as Sir Cuthbert, waving a languid hand, said in his own brutally indifferent fashion, "I am told she is half starved."

Emma, unwrapping the baby, shot him a furious look. Then she stared down at Mara, and it seemed to her—though it was probably just her imagining—that the little eyes opened a slit and Mara stared back in appeal. At the same time she kicked her feet with surprising energy and let out an angry yowl.

God help her, the little one had a stout heart! Well, if God hadn't helped her, then Emma must. Angus would understand. She pulled off the shawl, untied the loose bed jacket she was wearing, and slipped a full blue-veined breast out of her gown and into the baby's mouth. After a few false starts the baby understood what was expected and began to suck vigorously.

By the time Angus came in for lunch and explanations, Sir Cuthbert was gone, and the new baby and Nurse had been installed in the room with two-year-old Duggie and Emma's baby Donnie.

"I know what you're thinking, Angus," said Emma, seeing his shadowed face. "And you're wrong. This has nothing to do with Sir Cuthbert, nor even with the wee mite's being half-sister to our Duggie. She could have been anyone's! She's a day-old baby and she was *hungry*! How could I turn her away . . . me with enough milk to feed half the babies in the county and still have something left over for those across the border in Dumfriesshire? And you, you tenderhearted one, you'd not refuse suck to a starving calf, let alone a baby. Especially one—if half what Nurse has to say is true—as unlucky in her mother as in her father!"

"But I'll not take his money!"

"I already told him so," Emma agreed with satisfaction. "But he *will* pay Nurse's wages . . . that's only right. And she'll be a help to me with Donnie and Duggie, too, which I'll need sorely after Mam leaves. I don't mind admitting, they tire me, your sons do." She leaned up against him. "You take the energy out of your womenfolk, it's the way of men," she told him teasingly.

He scooped her up and sat down with her on his lap. Emma twined her arms around his neck and sighed in satisfaction.

"Whist, lass!" he said, his green eyes twinkling. "You're not the light armful you used to be. Do you think it's all that rich milk weighting you down?"

He kissed her neck, adding soberly, "It's in neither of us to turn away a hungry child. Let the little lassie stay then so long as she needs us."

So it was the "little lassie," instead of being brought up at Rydale Park, as the pampered and unwanted daughter of Lady Mary Kendal and Sir Cuthbert Rydale, was lovingly reared at Treeways Cottage by Emma MacTavish, ex-mistress, former parlor maid, caring mother, farmer's wife.

Chapter Five

NEIGHBORS—TAKING THEIR CUE FROM EMMA and Angus MacTavish, who treated all three children alike, bestowing kisses and cuffs, as the occasion demanded, with a fine impartiality—called them the MacTavish litter.

In looks they were as different as could be. Douglas, always called Duggie, had his mother's mop of russet hair and her merry brown eyes. The hair and the eyes were what people noticed, seldom seeing that the face framed by the rioting hair had the lean aristocratic features cropping up in Rydale family portraits for six generations, a nose long enough to seem disdainful, high cheekbones, and a prominent chin.

Donald, never called anything but Donnie, was Angus all over again, a sturdy muscular boy, serious and dependable, with the saving

43

grace and humor of his father as well as his candid face and appealing green eyes.

Mara would have seemed a changeling in any family she belonged to—Rydale, Kendal, or MacTavish. She had eyes dark as midnight, mysterious and ever-changing as the waters of the river Eden in which she played so often and so disobediently. No matter how many times Emma confined her hair—which was thick and black and straight as that of an Indian princess—in ribbons or in braids, it invariably wound up over her shoulders or down her back in a mass of tangles. Her nose and her cheekbones and her chin were remarkably like Duggie's, but again, most people noticed the hair and eyes and unconsciously attributed them to her being "really a Rydale."

No eighteenth-century Kendal was aware of the Castilian sailor who had managed to reach shore during the invasion attempt of the Spanish Armada. Hidden in a fisherman's cave by the unhappily married wife of an unknown Kendal, he had been discovered and properly disposed of by a band of patriotic and zealous Englishmen—but not without first presenting a token of his gratitude to the distressed lady that would leave a permanent mark on succeeding generations.

Mara knew that she was "really a Rydale," because that was her name, and it was the name of the cold, contained man and the pretty, fluttering woman who visited her three or four times a year, bringing baskets of fine things to eat and boxes full of presents and, at the same time, spreading such an air of unease all through the cottage that she, as well as the others, was intensely glad to see them leave again.

Mara knew that the man and the woman were her true "Mama" and "Papa," and, instructed by Emma, she used those words in their presence, but the words had no real meaning. As soon as their visit was over, Emma and Angus turned into Mam and Da again, and Mara's world became safe.

She knew that it was thanks to "Mama" and "Papa" that she and Duggie and Donnie had their bay colt, Tartan, to ride and a cart and donkey of their own as well as Nurse to fuss over them and help Mam in the house.

She tried dutifully to be grateful, but somehow she couldn't be. Somehow she knew the pretty lady didn't really like her. The pretty lady in her silks and laces, whose hair sometimes hung down her neck in fat yellow curls and at other times was piled high on her head and unaccountably powdered like Emma's pie dough, always seemed uncomfortable in Mara's presence.

The man wasn't uncomfortable . . . he was indifferent. He said things like, "You obviously feed her well . . . she's growing like a weed." Or, with an unpleasantly laughing sidelong look at the pretty lady, "Those dark gypsy looks remind me of a lady I used to know in Arabia."

Mara, who was clever and quicksilver at all other times, lapsed into a state of dull docility on these visits, even as her midnight eyes darted back and forth, missing nothing. She noticed not only that the lady shrank from her presence, let alone her touch, but that the man looked at Duggie more often than he did at her. He looked at Duggie the way Duggie had looked at the apple pie his mother put on the window to cool, saying it was for the Widow Newsome . . . with a kind of hungry yearning.

Mara didn't begrudge Duggie that look. She had no desire for the man to yearn over her, and it was only natural he should feel that way about Duggie.

To Mara, Mam and Da were love and strength and security. Nurse, of course, was added warmth and comfort. Donnie was her own dear five-hours-older brother. The bay colt, Tartan, the donkey, Whist, and their dog, Lad, were the dearest possessions they all had together; but Duggie was life's best gift. There was no one in the whole wide world like him. He was completely wonderful, and she loved him with all her heart.

If Angus was around, he always left the house during the "visits." He couldn't abide the Rydales . . . not because of what had once been between his wife and Sir Cuthbert (he felt sure and secure of his Emma), but because they had farmed out their child long after the need was there, disposed of her like a piece of unwanted livestock.

Emma endured the visits, but she no longer feared them. In the early days, when the baby Mara had become as dear to her as the two she had birthed, she was gripped by fear whenever the Rydale carriage appeared, even if it contained no Rydales, only gifts or a message.

She suckled the baby long after she should have been weaned, so as to be able to say that Mara still needed her. Nurse aided and abetted this scheme wholeheartedly. She wanted to stay with Mara at Treeways Cottage forever.

Angus knew what the women were up to and said nothing. If *they* at Rydale wanted the "wee lassie," *they* would take her, come what may. His heart contracted with pain at the very thought, for he, too, had taken her into that organ as well as into his house.

Gradually, they all came to realize that Rydale Park was just as content with the arrangement as Treeways Cottage. Emma weaned the baby. Outsiders almost forgot that Mara had not been born a MacTavish.

Then, when Mara was six years old, her mother died in childbirth along with a second daughter. The funeral was planned on the same grand scale as the late Sir Oliver's obsequies, and Mara and Nurse were sent for.

Emma wept and Nurse wailed and, the atmosphere proving contagious, Mara and the boys did both till Angus took a hand.

"Whist now, you're frightening the bairns," he said, shooing all three "bairns" out of the house.

"Will you stop acting so daft, the both of you!" he expostulated to the women when the children had run happily out of doors. "It's just a visit. She'll be back within the week."

"How can you be sure?" Emma asked him tearfully. "Now that Lady Mary is gone, he may want Mara back."

"Use your head, woman. It's a son he still wants. He'll be looking about him for a new wife before the poor lady is cold. He won't want to be bothered with the lassie."

"Then why did he send for her?"

"All his family is gathering. She's family too. It's for the appearance of the thing. He'll want her handy in the house when she's sent for to meet members of the clan." He turned toward Nurse. "Tell her it's so, Nurse."

Nurse had brightened amazingly during this speech. "You know, Emma," she said slowly, "I think Mr. MacTavish may be in the right of it. You must remember from your time of working in the Great House the store they set by doing the right thing."

"The right thing," Emma sniffed, but she, too, cheered and was able to send Mara off in her father's carriage without further tears.

As soon as they arrived at Rydale—since Sir Cuthbert would not permit Mara to be installed in the suite new-furnished for the long-awaited heir—Nurse went upstairs to see to the old nursery rooms, hastily set to rights by Amy and Louise, still weeping for their poor, pretty, silly mistress.

Mara was escorted to the library by Handley, now very old and bent, to see her father. Although Sir Cuthbert was dressed conventionally in deep black, his face was most improperly cheerful.

He greeted his small daughter with a bow, as though she were a morning visitor, waved her to a seat in a comfortable armchair, and addressed Handley. "Some refreshment for Miss Rydale."

Mara looked about her and then realized that *she* was Miss Rydale.

Sir Cuthbert seated himself opposite her. "You were told, I believe, that your mama, Lady Mary, is dead?"

Mara nodded solemnly.

"You're very sad, I suppose?"

"It's sad to be dead," Mara agreed. Feeling by his silence that something more was called for, after a slight pause she added, "I was *very* sad when Ophelia got dead."

"Who, pray, is or was Ophelia?"

"Ophelia was my kitten, my *first* kitten. I have another one now, a boy kitten."

"Your family is gathering soon to drown you in sympathy and sentiment. I trust that your remarks to its members will be more tactful, if less honest."

"Sir?" asked Mara bewilderedly.

"However much you mourn your kitten and how little you mourn your mother—most understandably," Sir Cuthbert murmured with gentle irony, "when strangers ask, you must merely say that, yes, you are very sad. You need not weep," he added cynically. "They will do all the weeping for you."

Handley came in with a tray and set it on a small table beside Mara. She looked with pleasure at the tall glass of milk and the big plate of sweet cakes. "Thank you, sir," she said in her friendly way.

Sir Cuthbert frowned, but Handley beamed. "You are more than welcome, Miss Mara," he said, bowing to her.

"My daughter," Sir Cuthbert instructed her when Handley left the room, "does not address servants as 'sir.'"

"But M—Emma says I must be respectful to my elders."

"It is for servants to be respectful to *you*. Well, never mind that now." He waved irritably. "Drink your milk. Eat. Do you understand what I said to you before?"

Mara crunched down on a pastry, her dark,

changeable eyes alive with intelligence. "I must not talk about Ophelia, and I will be very sad my mama is dead," she said matter-of-factly.

"Quickness of comprehension from your mother's daughter. Amazing. But then I suppose . . . however reluctant . . . I must take some credit on myself."

Mara stared at him over the rim of her glass. It seemed to her that even while he was telling *her* to show sadness, he was making it plain that he hadn't liked the pretty, silly lady who was "Mama" any more than she had.

He wasn't a very kind man, she decided suddenly, not in the least like Angus. Angus was so very gentle with helpless creatures, two-legged as well as four. Even when he punished his children, they instinctively knew he was not being unkind. His easy humor was never directed to hurting people.

She stood up, setting down the glass.

"Would you like me to go to Nurse now, sir?" she asked politely.

He raised his eyebrows superciliously. "I am being dismissed? By all means, go to Nurse, and tell her to put on your mourning dress. Our guests will be arriving soon."

The Earl and Countess of Kendal and their only unmarried daughter, Lady Margaret, were the first of the expected guests to arrive. A message was sent up to the nursery wing and Nurse brought Mara to the drawing room to greet them.

She was wearing the new dress that had been provided for her. It was dark and ugly, Mara thought; even the crocheted lace collar was black.

The large weeping woman seated on the brocade sofa regarded this unrelieved mourning with approval. "Well, at least the child is dressed properly," she said waspishly. "Come and kiss me, girl; I'm your grandmother."

Mara hesitated, saw the significant jerk of Sir Cuthbert's head, and moved obediently, if on reluctant feet, to place a quick kiss on the rouged and powdered cheek.

"And this is your grandfather." She indicated the man standing near to her. "And this"—she touched the arm of the weeping young woman beside her—"is your Aunt Margaret."

Mara curtsied quickly, avoiding more kisses; and her father, with a faint smile, as though he had read her mind, indicated a hassock not too near to the sofa. She sat down on it gladly.

"Ever since we got word of our shocking loss," Lady Wordsworth said to Sir Cuthbert in a peculiarly penetrating voice, "we have been discussing what is best for dear Mara. It cannot be good for a child—a girl

—to be raised in a motherless household. I own it would be a sacrifice at my age to take on the responsibility, but I feel I owe it to the child as well as to my dear daughter's memory. . . ." Her tears fell again.

Sir Cuthbert, who was fully aware that Lady Wordsworth had raised her five daughters with nurses, maids, and governesses but little personal exertion, allowed himself a slight cynical smile.

"How much?" he asked.

"I beg your pardon."

"I asked how much your sacrifice will cost me."

Lord Wordsworth coughed. "You would naturally wish to pay her personal expenses, sir, a trifling amount."

"Her personal expenses are a trifling amount at present. I don't propose to increase them. You must be aware that Treeways Cottage, where she resides, is far from being a motherless household."

"You surely don't propose to leave her there . . . in a farmer's home? It is not fit."

"Your daughter was most content to have her reared at Treeways. She showed no inclination at all to bring her into *this* house. It seems to me the greatest respect I could show to Lady Mary's memory is to have my daughter raised in accordance with Lady Mary's wishes."

"I protest, sir," said the Earl of Kendal, very red-faced. "You cannot be—"

"Protest all you wish, my lord," Sir Cuthbert interrupted him quite rudely. "I shall not change my mind. Above all, I shall not be induced again to frank your debts, disguised this time as personal expenses for my daughter."

"You are insulting, sir!"

"You are, too, sir, when you take me for quite such a fool. I paid your debts once, my lord, to the tune of many thousands of pounds. I made a handsome settlement on your youngest daughter when we were wed and I bought husbands for three of the others. Lady Margaret"—he turned toward her courteously—"may not have wed, but neither, thanks to me, will she be destitute on your death when your estates revert to your distant cousin."

While the Earl of Kendal grew pale and his countess scarlet and Lady Margaret hid her pockmarked face behind her hands, Sir Cuthbert continued in cold, measured tones, "I swelled the Kendal coffers once, my lord, to marry and beget a son. Eight years. Eight, my lord, and what have I to show for them?"

In the shocked stillness of the room, his own answer to his question was uttered with all the fury of those same eight years of stored resentment. "I did not get so much as a halfpenny's worth out of the monies I spent, Lord Wordsworth. I will not be gulled again by the Kendals."

Mara sat trembling on her hassock. She almost wept with relief to hear Sir Cuthbert's final declaration. "After the funeral, the child returns to Treeways."

Chapter Six

SIX MONTHS AFTER HIS WIFE'S ENTOMBMENT, making no hypocritical pretense of regret, Sir Cuthbert put off his blacks. With his valet up beside him and two footmen and the trunks containing his new wardrobe of fashionable gray garments following behind, he proceeded on a slow and stately two-coach progress to London to choose a second wife.

During the half-year of his ostensible mourning, he had set the affairs of his estate in order for the months to come, spent many pleasurable evenings with Millie Sloan and even taken her on one brief visit across the border to Dumfriesshire to visit their son and daughter, who were fostered out to a Scottish gamekeeper and his wife.

Influenced more than he would have cared to think by the words of his late wife's mother, before his departure Sir Cuthbert also arranged for more proper schooling for his bastard son by Emma MacTavish and his daughter, Mara Rydale. Up till now the two, as well as Donnie, had learned their letters in haphazard fashion from an elderly spinster piano teacher who came to Treeways twice a week.

The vicar's curate, an Oxford scholar with too little money and too many small mouths to feed, was almost tearfully grateful for the opportunity to turn his small study into a permanent day school for "the MacTavish litter."

Although Sir Cuthbert had only made provision for two pupils, the curate, Mr. Newcastle, made no demur when the donkey cart pulled up in front of the door of his tiny house, disgorging three.

Emma MacTavish had no intention of seeing one of her "bairns" treated any differently from the others. No extra money was ever mentioned, but weekly a stream of gifts flowed between Treeways and the curate's cottage. Fresh fruits and vegetables, eggs, chickens, on special occasions a goose or duck, and at curing times a side of bacon, a slab of ham, or some choice mutton.

Life at the curate's cottage improved tremendously for his own little family after he established his school; and Mr. Newcastle derived the born teacher's satisfaction of opening three bright inquiring minds to the knowledge contained in his beloved books.

Duggie was the most intelligent of the

three, Mr. Newcastle soon decided, which was a good thing, as Sir Cuthbert had decreed that in a few years' time he must be prepared to enter a proper public school. He absorbed all that he was taught—Greek, Latin, mathematics, literature—with a kind of effortless ease that made his polite disinterest all the more regrettable.

The only subject that truly fascinated him was history, particularly military history. "When I'm old enough," Duggie told Mr. Newcastle matter-of-factly, "I'm going to go for a soldier. I'll be an officer in one of His Majesty's best regiments."

Mr. Newcastle stroked his smooth chin and politely refrained from expressing his inward reflection that farmers' sons—even those befriended by a baronet out of gratitude to his daughter's foster parents—did not commonly receive commissions in good regiments.

Donnie was helpless at Greek and Latin but brilliant at mathematics and the natural sciences. Mr. Newcastle wisely decided that it was foolish to waste the boy's time with the classics, where neither his inclinations nor his future lay—Donnie only wanted to be a farmer like his Da—and allowed him to pursue his own interests.

For Mara, Mr. Newcastle had prepared the easiest curriculum of all. She, too, would go to school one day, her father had indicated, to learn the usual foolishness that was called education for a young lady. All Mr. Newcastle was required to do for her was to make her acceptable to such a school.

Mara, learning of the simple course of study planned for her, threw one of her rare fits of temper. She would learn what Duggie was learning, she declared—stamping one small foot. The book of *Rules for Little Ladies* was thrown scornfully across the study.

Having birched her hand (so gently she hardly felt the three strokes) for this unseemly display, the curate (who could not find it in his heart to blame even a female's exhibiting a thirst for knowledge) agreed that Miss Mara might study the same subjects as the older MacTavish boy.

Outside of Mr. Newcastle's study, the boys were brought up no differently than other farmers' sons. They learned to milk, to help put in the crops and harvest them, to tend sheep, curry horses, and mend fences.

Mara was required to gather the eggs, feed the chickens, and assist Emma and Nurse in the house. She was always reminded that she was a Rydale and would be the fine lady of her own household one day.

"Still," Emma invariably wound up this admonition, "I'll not have you the kind of helpless creature passing for a lady who knows how to *pour* a cup of tea elegantly but couldn't *brew* one to save her life."

And when Mara grumbled at being put to polish Mam's few rare precious pieces of silver, Emma would tell her tartly, "Someday when you have servants, I hope you'll remember your feelings now and treat them like human beings."

Mr. Newcastle's study-school continued, except for holidays, uninterrupted and untroubled for five happy years.

During that time Mara was only once summoned home to Rydale . . . during the first summer after her father returned to the Park with his London bride.

Again Emma and Nurse spent the time between the summons and her departure dissolved in tears, but Mara only laughed and, like a donkey switching its tail, tossed her mane of shining blue-black hair back over her shoulders.

"Don't worry, Mam. If they try to keep me, I'll run away home," she promised with her own remarkable self-assurance.

"More like, you'll make life so miserable for them at Rydale, the poor folk will be thankful to send you back to us," said Angus dryly.

Mara grinned across at him. "That's a fine idea, Da!" she told him perkily.

She was prepared to do just that, if she had to, but it wasn't necessary.

The new Lady Rydale was a kindly, good-natured woman in most respects, but she considered it bad enough to have to stare every night at her predecessor in the drawing room without having this exceptionally lovely looking stepdaughter living underfoot as well.

The first Lady Rydale had been painted in the first year of her marriage, looking utterly young and beautiful; her portrait still hung over the fireplace purely because Sir Cuthbert never noticed it. The second Lady Rydale, jealous and insecure, was afraid to bring it to his notice.

Although Sir Cuthbert's new wife came of a moderately prominent family and was possessed of an ample if not overlarge dowry, she was four and twenty, not only unwed when he first set eyes on her but also unsought.

Her face, though not unpleasant, was rather long and narrow, dominated by wide lips, with a mouthful of white but overlarge teeth. Her voice was unusually deep and so was her rather neighing laugh.

Miss Griselda Langhorne, some jokester had declared at her come-out party six years before, not only looked like a horse, she laughed like one. The cruel jest had passed quickly around the ballroom and from there filtered down to all of fashionable London.

It became the fashion to laugh at Miss Langhorne, not to court her; and when she proved to be a masterful horsewoman, rather than earning praise for her, the joke was somehow improved on.

Within two weeks of his arrival in London, Sir Cuthbert's speculative glance had landed on Griselda Langhorne at a private party and he was inquiring of Miss Hillcrest, the pretty dinner partner on his right, "Who is that young lady two down and across from us, the one with the brown braids and—"

"And the mouthful of teeth?" Miss Hillcrest broke in helpfully. "You must mean the brown mare?"

"I beg your pardon."

"That's what she's called in London society, 'the brown mare,'" giggled Miss Hillcrest, secure in her own good looks. "Because she's so horse-faced, you know, and even laughs like a horse and looks like one in . . . well, in the back, too. Out six years, poor thing, and she's never had a beau."

Sir Cuthbert, not a kind person himself, looked at his dinner companion with distaste. He could picture his late unlamented wife making just such a speech. Lord, how he had grown to despise pretty, insipid, useless creatures like this one!

When the gentlemen were done with their drinking and rejoined the ladies in the drawing room, Cuthbert passed by Miss Hillcrest with just a brief bow, despite her warmly welcoming nods and smiles.

He advanced to a part of the room where, while conversing with some older gentleman, he could study "the brown mare." She had a trim waist curving out in wide hips, which were no doubt what Miss Hillcrest had reference to when she described her as looking like a horse "in the back."

Well—never mind current fashion—Sir Cuthbert Rydale had no objection to wide hips. In fact, he rated them rather higher, he realized dispassionately, than skinny flanks that were no sport for a man during childmaking as well as no good to a woman for childbearing.

Sir Cuthbert drew nearer to Miss Langhorne's circle; she was talking animatedly to the three men grouped near to her. He could hear her voice . . . her laugh . . . and found he had no objection to either. On the contrary, it was the tinkling light laughs, the small squeaky voices like Lady Mary's and Miss Hillcrest's, he had come to abhor.

A dowager he approached was happy to inform him that the three gentlemen with Miss Langhorne were her married brothers. "She has three younger ones still at school."

"Six brothers!" Sir Cuthbert was impressed. "How many sisters?"

"None. Boys seem to run in all the Langhorne family connections."

"*Do* they?" murmured Sir Cuthbert. Then, "I should like to meet the young lady, ma'am, if you would be so kind as to introduce me."

Another man might have studied her face when the introduction took place. Sir Cuthbert had already done so at the dinner table. The part of her anatomy on which he feasted his eyes, even as he uttered commonplace courtesies, was the bosom overflowing her tight bodice.

Sir Cuthbert had never forgotten the sight of Emma MacTavish suckling first her own son and then his daughter. For the first time since that memorable morning he was beholding breasts to compare with Emma's. This pair looked bountiful enough to nourish an entire orphanage.

"I understand, Miss Langhorne," Sir Cuthbert said almost immediately after he had maneuvered her away from the cluster of her brothers, "that you are a superior horsewoman."

A quick, scared look slanted upward reassured Griselda that he was not making mock of her.

"Yes," she said simply.

"I would be honored to escort you for a ride in the park one morning."

Griselda gaped up at him. No man since her come-out, except one of her brothers, had ever asked her to ride with him. No man had ever sent her flowers or invited her to the opera or a play. Seldom, unless coerced by a determined hostess, had one requested the honor of a dance. She had given up attending balls midway during her first season, rather than sit among the chaperones, her lips sore from the effort of being continually curved in a smile as insincere as it was silly, while she waited in vain to be asked.

"Will you ride with me, ma'am?" repeated

Sir Cuthbert, unexpectedly touched by the soft, vulnerable brown eyes and big, drooping mouth.

"Oh yes, I would be so pleased!" she gasped out.

They fixed on the morning after the next one, and by the time that first ride was over, Sir Cuthbert had made up his mind.

Miss Griselda Langhorne looked elegant, if not handsome, in a plain russet-brown riding dress that was much more suited to her figure and her style than fussier formal dress.

She rode superbly, displaying on the back of a horse all the skill and assurance that she lacked in a drawing room.

Coaxed out of her initial shyness, she could speak easily and sensibly, yet seemed to know how to be comfortably silent as well.

Her person was not displeasing; she should make a pleasant, easy companion. She was neither too young nor too old, and with those hips and those breasts . . .

Six brothers, Sir Cuthbert kept telling himself on that first of many rides . . .

He would have his son at last!

Chapter Seven

THE EVENING OF MARA'S ARRIVAL, WHILE THE new Lady Rydale's maid was preparing her for bed, Griselda suffered a fit of remorse for all the unkind thoughts she had been nourishing toward her poor motherless stepdaughter. She resolved to go down to the breakfast room early and make amends to the poor thing.

She would be a friend to her, she decided determinedly. "*And* a mother, too," she said aloud even more valiantly, and then gave a tiny sigh.

She was five months married by now and had hoped to be pregnant long before this, but thus far there wasn't the slightest sign to give her hope.

She gave an even deeper sigh. She did *so* want to be pregnant. She knew full well her dear Cuthbert had married her to beget a son, and with all her heart she longed to oblige him in return for all he had given her.

Her feeling for him had begun as ardent gratitude during their brief period of courtship. After their hurried wedding, his skill as a lover had awakened the core of passion that none but he had ever suspected was lying dormant in her, yearning to be released.

"The brown mare," no longer a whipping girl for the wits of London but the respected wife of Sir Cuthbert Rydale, had fallen deeply in love with her formidable forty-year-old husband.

Unfortunately for Griselda's good intentions, Sir Cuthbert came to her room that night and they were so well pleased with one another, he not only remained in her bed but turned to her again in the morning. It was well past eleven before they both went down to breakfast, and Miss Mara, Handley informed them, had breakfasted hours before and gone for a walk.

Griselda suppressed a pang of guilt as she poured out coffee for Sir Cuthbert, adding just the amount of sugar and cream that he liked.

"Does Mara ride?" she asked.

Sir Cuthbert shrugged carelessly. "I provided a horse for her. I assume she does."

"Well, if not, I could teach her," Griselda said resolutely. "I may not have many skills, but that is certainly one I can impart."

Sir Cuthbert put down his knife and fork and pinched her chin gently between the thumb and index finger of his right hand. "You must not speak *so*," he chided.

"S-s-sir?" she stammered.

"You have *many* skills, you please *me* in all ways, and I will not allow anyone—even you—to speak disparagingly of the woman whom I am honored to call wife."

These were the most tender words Sir Cuthbert had ever spoken in his life, certainly the most loving that Griselda had ever heard addressed to her. She sat in stunned silence for a moment, slow, happy tears rolling down her cheeks. Sir Cuthbert took one of her limp hands in his and pressed it to his lips before picking up his fork and glancing at his newspaper.

Happiness gave new impetus to Griselda's resolution to be a good stepmother. A little while later, in the drawing room, she said steadfastly to her husband, "I think it would be proper for Mara to live with us now, do you not?"

"If you wish it," Sir Cuthbert returned carelessly.

"She's a charming child . . . and very lovely looking," Griselda continued determinedly. She looked up at the portrait over the mantel, swallowing hard. "She doesn't at all resemble her mother, does she?"

Sir Cuthbert's eyes followed the direction

of hers. "No, she does not; thank God for small mercies," he said caustically.

"Th-thank G-God," Griselda echoed incredulously. "But I thought . . . I thought . . ."

Sir Cuthbert looked at her intently. "What did you think, my dear?"

"She was so very beautiful," his wife said barely above a whisper. "I thought you were madly in love with her."

"She *was* very beautiful," Sir Cuthbert acknowledged dryly, "if one likes Dresden shepherdesses, which I do not. But *entre nous,* my dear, a quarter-hour of her company was more wearying than a full day's hunt." He gave her a sudden charming smile. "And however ungentlemanly it may be to remark it, I must confess she was even more deadly dull in the bedroom than in the parlor."

As Griselda sat, speechless with surprise and delight, he inquired curiously, "What made you think I was enamored of her, my lady?"

"Her p-p-portrait," Griselda stammered. "You still have it hanging . . ." Her voice trailed off; she could only point.

"Good God!" said Sir Cuthbert, gazing blankly up at the portrait. "So I do. How very remiss of me, my sweet."

Saying which, he yanked vigorously at the bell pull.

Handley appeared a moment later.

Sir Cuthbert waved a negligent hand toward the portrait over the mantel. "Handley, see to it that the painting of Lady Mary is removed sometime today and the Turner landscape put in its place."

"But what shall I do with Lady Mary, Sir Cuthbert?" Handley asked in shock.

"Consign it to one of the attics. Well, no"—seeing the small reproving shake of Griselda's head—"I suppose you can't do that. Have it put in the art gallery, man."

When Handley had tottered out, "Do you feel better, my dear?" he asked Griselda.

"I'm ashamed to admit that I do."

"Why ashamed?"

"I was jealous of her," Griselda answered with disarming simplicity.

"Good God! You! Jealous of her!" He tweaked so vigorously at the coronet of braids wound about her head that one brown braid came tumbling down her back.

"If she were alive, the reverse might be justified," he told his "brown mare" so soberly that tears of joy rolled down her face again as she went in search of Mara.

She found her stepdaughter in the woods back of the garden and, wrapped in the golden glow of her own happiness, went straight to the point with an offer of the most wonderful gift it was in her power to give.

"Mara, your father and I think that you should make your home with us."

Mara sprang up from the patch of grass where she had been sitting, picking daisies. "I won't!" she told Griselda mutinously.

Her stepmother's mouth opened wide in astonishment, revealing the two horselike rows of teeth. "What did you say?"

Mara cursed her impulsive tongue. Hadn't Emma cautioned her over and over that treacle was much more likely to attract insects than vinegar? She stood up, bobbing a respectful curtsy. "I mean, it's very kind of you, ma'am, but I would rather go home."

"But this *is* your home."

"That's *ridikalous*." Mara spoke up scornfully. "Nurse took me away from here the day I was borned and I didn't come back till my mama got dead, and then again yesterday."

"Oh," said Griselda faintly. "I didn't know."

"It's not your fault," Mara told her fairmindedly, "but home is with Mam—I mean, with Emma and Angus. Home is where Duggie and Donnie and Nurse are."

"You mean that you are happier at Treeways than you would be here?"

"Oh, yes." Looking up into the kind, homely face staring down at her in some dismay, Mara decided in a sudden burst of contrition that she had, perhaps, not been too tactful. Hadn't Mam shaken her head more times than Mara could count while she mentioned ruefully, "When the good fairy came down to

71

earth to hand out tact, my lass, she surely flew over your cradle!"

"It's awfully kind of you to ask me, Lady Rydale, ma'am, and you're very welcome to visit me at Treeways, but please, I would rather go home."

"Then you shall," said Griselda firmly. "Just remember this is your *second* home . . . so if you change your mind, you have only to let me know. And I think, since I can't be either your mama or your mam, you had better call me Griselda. Lady Rydale is much too formal."

She smiled, and Mara smiled; and they were suddenly friends, all the better friends for being so soon to part.

A message was dispatched to Treeways to reassure Emma that her beloved nursling would be home by the end of the week, and, secure in this knowledge, Mara could enjoy the four or five days left of her visit.

She spent most of her afternoons with Griselda, who admired her prowess riding a horse astride or even bareback, but suggested that since, in a few years, she would not be allowed to appear publicly on anything except a sidesaddle, she had better learn to ride one now. The older she got, the harder it would be.

Mara despised the sidesaddle as unwieldy, horrid, and—in her favorite word— ridikalous, but having gained her main point, she was anxious to please her step-mother in lesser ones.

When Mara determined to do a thing, she did it well. By the end of the week, Griselda was boasting to Sir Cuthbert of how well his daughter rode.

Since, again at Griselda's behest, she was bidden to the dinner table every night instead of having her meals in the nursery, Mara saw more of her father than she ever had before. At first she was unenthused about the honor. Later she decided he was less grim than he used to be, his tongue not so biting as she remembered. He laughed far more often, even teased his women at table almost as they did at Treeways.

It was because, thought Mara wisely, studying the two with bright, watchful eyes, Sir Cuthbert liked Griselda so much better than he had her poor pretty mama. She found herself unexpectedly experiencing a pang of pity for that silly, unappreciated lady whose portrait no longer hung over the drawing room mantel.

Sir Cuthbert seemed impressed by his daughter's easy manners, mettlesome spirit, and above all, her lively intelligence.

In spite of all these pluses, however, when the week's successful visit was over, Griselda was delighted to be alone again with her beloved husband and Mara was overjoyed to return to her true family at Treeways.

Chapter Eight

MARA CRIED FOR TWO DAYS AND TWO NIGHTS when Duggie was sent to school at Eton in faraway Berkshire.

Angus finally marched her off to the barn, where they could be alone and he could tell her seriously, "All of life is change, lass, and you had best become accustomed to it soon as late or a sad, sorry row you'll have to hoe in years to come."

"Why can't things go on as they are?" Mara wept in the age-old cry of a child who wants her world safe and the same.

"Because time doesn't stand still, love, and neither do people. Even if our Duggie stayed home, before long *you* would be the one to leave. Your father—quite rightly—wants you to go to school to learn the ways of a lady that you won't acquire at Treeways."

"I don't want to be a lady!"

"It's not your choice, my lass, or even ours.

Not that I think it a bad thing. You aren't going to be a boy-girl all your life, and since you can't wed with a farmer, it's best you learn the things a gentleman will expect you to know."

Not daring to indicate her opinion of this philosophizing in English, which she knew would earn her a hearty smack on the backside, Mara made a rude remark in Latin. Angus—nobody's fool, even if his knowledge of Latin could have been stuffed with room to spare inside Emma's silver thimble—judged her answer by tone, not words, and gave her the smack anyway.

"You don't even know what I said!" Mara accused him bitterly as she rubbed her smarting bottom, feeling doubly injured by this injustice.

"Don't I, though?" Angus retorted. "You keep a civil tongue in your head, my girl, or you'll be off to that school even sooner than we planned."

Mara subsided and from that moment on saved her tears for bed. Not that there were many. Her naturally buoyant spirits soon restored her to cheerfulness and optimism. Letters streamed back and forth between Eton and Treeways, and big boxes stuffed with all the foodstuffs that would survive the journey traveled one-way.

His boxes from home, Duggie wrote cheerfully, were the envy of all his House. He not only used their contents to supplement the meager meals for himself and friends, and some for treats for the juniors, but also judiciously doled out bribes to the senior boys.

"It's saved my hide lots of times," he wrote matter-of-factly in one letter home. His first private letter to Mara was more explicit.

God, but I'm thankful not to have been sent here younger like so many of these poor little sods, who are bullied and beaten unmercifully by the older boys, let alone the masters.

Keate, the headmaster, is kind by comparison, even though he's known as a famous flogger, but that's more because of the number of boys he goes through in a single day rather than the strokes he doles out—never more than five with a single birch or, if you're really for it, ten with two.

You'll find this hard to believe, but they turn the flogging sessions into social events. There's usually a large attendance, especially if the victims are known to put on a good show. It's greatly appreciated if they yell and shout and carry on even though they're not much hurt. The bystanders yell, too, and applaud the best performances. Can't see much fun in it myself.

In another letter he expressed gratitude that Sir Cuthbert, his patron, had paid the extra six guineas the year to get him a single bed and room to himself.

"With some of the things that go on here, it's more necessary than you might think," he wrote cryptically.

"Whatever does he mean by that, Da?" Mara inquired curiously, interrupting Donnie, who was reading the letter aloud to the whole family assembled at the lunch table.

They all—Mara, Donnie, Emma, Nurse—looked at Angus, their source of all practical knowledge. His face took on the blank look that Emma knew meant it was a subject to be spoken of only in the privacy of their bedroom.

"Whist now," he said casually, "we'll have to ask him when he comes home. Go on with the letter, Donnie."

Donnie read on.

This will make you laugh, but the only other boy in our form who has a single room is Lord Raleigh Irwine, the youngest son of the Duke of Ghent. Can you fancy it . . . me and a duke's son having the same privileges?

Happen we'd be neighbors if the Irwines ever came to Cumberland because the noble duke owns Dumfries, you know, Da, the big newish castle and the huge estate our side of the border near Carlisle that you said had the worst-off tenants because his Grace never goes near the property himself.

I admit I was a bit set against any son of Ghent's at first, but I soon realized it wasn't fair to blame him for his father's neglect and he's the best of all the chaps I've met.

He was first sent here when he was only seven, so that means he's been here more than half his life (he's ten months older than me). Some of his stories of how he was treated in the early days would make your hair stand up on end (not yours, Mara, yours is always on end). But he learned to rough it out and has the reputation of being quite a prankster even though the one tease he won't stand for himself is any reference to spreading out capes, the way Sir Walter Raleigh was supposed to have done for Queen Elizabeth. He insists on being called Roy.

Whenever the Baffin (that's the name they give Keate here) summons Roy to the library for the usual, it's pretty sure to be because he punched the head—or tried to—of someone who called him Sir Walter.

Every letter after that contained some anecdote about Roy Irwine. Mara went through shifting emotions about her idol's "best friend." First she was jealous, then curious, then amused. Before long she was looking forward as eagerly as the rest of her family to each new story.

The weather can be wild and stormy [wrote Duggie in November] but no Etonian is ever permitted to indulge in the weakness of sheltering under an umbrella, even though Keate himself—rain or shine—is never seen abroad without one. He mostly seems to use it as a weapon, poking the point at any boy he comes across.

Roy bought an umbrella and waited till one day when it was happening to mizzle ever so slightly. Then he went outdoors, put up his umbrella, and strolled along—minced, I should say—making sure, of course, to put himself in the Baffin's way.

"You, sir! You there! What are you doing with that umbrella?" Keate roared out.

"Me, sir?" asked Roy, looking about him in pretended bewilderment, as though a score of boys might be about with their umbrellas instead of only him (though a half dozen of us were crouched in doorways and a full dozen hanging from the windows, all of us holding back our mirth).

"Yes, you, sir. Why do you carry an umbrella?" shouted Keate even as he jabbed the point of his own into the middle button of Roy's jacket.

Roy put out his free hand and two random raindrops fell onto it. "It rains, sir," he said affectedly. "I was protecting my health." He put the same hand to his chest. "I have a cough, sir."

He proceeded to cough in exact imitation of the baa-ing, barking cough which first led to Keate's being known as the Baffin.

"Rain, sir. A cough, sir. Do you think this is a ladies' seminary that you carry an umbrella? If I see you with one again, I'll flog you, sir."

And off goes Keate, coughing and baa-ing and carrying his own umbrella. Which should have ended it on a fine hilarious note, only the next day when we came to Prose*, we all saw a big sign hanging from the ceiling. It bore the inscription, *Miss Keate, Ladies' Headmistress*.

The Baffin pulled down the sign, ripped it in two, and roared out the name of Lord Raleigh Irwine.

Roy stood up beside me in the back row.

"Did you put up this sign, sir?"

"No, sir, I did not, sir," Roy answered, in truth (so he told me later) and with some regret (because he hadn't thought of it).

"I don't believe you, sir. I see guilt in your eye." Keate smiled in the genial way he has as he issues the invitation to a flogging. "You will stay at eleven, sir."

Roy was pretty cheerful when he came

---

*Etonese for "prayers"

back from the library. "He evened up with me for the umbrella," he told me not unhappily. Then he winked. "But don't worry. I have a plan to go him one better."

I've been after him for days to tell me the plan, but he just smiles mysteriously and says I'll see soon enough.

The letter proceeded on with his own affairs, but for once Mara was less concerned with these than with Roy.

"Oh, I do wonder what his plan is." She looked thoughtful. "Now, what would *I* do if I were him?"

"It's sure to be a daft plan," said Emma, laughing.

"It's cruel the way they treat young boys," contributed Nurse.

"I'll take the farm any day," Donnie told them gratefully.

"He's foolish, yon Roy, but mettlesome," pronounced Angus.

They all waited even more eagerly than usual for Duggie's next letter.

"I know you're all agog to hear if and how Roy carried out his threat," he began his letter teasingly, "but you'll just have to hear about my doings first."

He proceeded for two pages to tell them about "his doings." Starting on the top of page three, he had scribbled a poem he titled "The Defeat of Keate."

LOVING LONGEST

On a day in December
(Which all Eton will remember)
Lord Raleigh Irwine was commanded by
  Keate
To report to the library in order to be beat.

It was a busy day for Keate on Execution
  Dock,
Seven victims went ahead of Irwine to the
  Block.
The capacity crowd that filled the room was
  quiet as in church
When his lordship bent forward and Keate
  unfurled the birch.

A single stroke landed, there was a common
  sigh;
Then picture the amazement as Roy's body
  rose on high.
It whirled, it gyrated, it spun there in
  space
Before Roy landed feet away, a smile upon his
  face.

No other than the Baffin helped Lord Raleigh
  to his feet
With an air of great solicitude, he urged a
  fast retreat.
"I must have touched a nerve, my lord,
An apology you deserve, my lord.
I think it best
You go home and rest,

But call a physician should you feel
  untoward,
Call on me if you should need, my lord."

A friend on either side of him (and one of the
  friends was me),
Lord Raleigh tottered from the room,
  convulsed by silent glee,
Which he managed to restrain till he got
  outside the door,
His place in Eton history secured
  forevermore.

When our grandsons' grandsons go to school
  one day
They will still be told the story of that
  marvelous day
At Eton
When Lord Raleigh Irwine, by a gymnick feat
Brought about
Its most famous rout,
The defeat
Of Keate
And the block—without a beating!

  That's what it was [Duggie's letter continued exuberantly], a gymnick feat. My
madman friend actually hired a professional
gymnastick performer he encountered at a
country fair to teach him how to make that
great leap in the air from the classic position.
He kept practising in his room till he was

sure he had gotten it perfectly. Needless to say, he is presently the hero of Eton, and if the Baffin has caught on yet, he is wisely pretending ignorance. While the supposed injured warrior was presumably resting on his bed of pain that night, practically the whole of our form was having a champagne and tea celebration in his room.

Dear Lord Raleigh [wrote Mara],

I hope you will enjoy eating the fruitcake I am sending to you. It is for the next feast in your room. Or anything else you want. Mam helped me to make it, so it should be good.

We all did so enjoy the story of how you got the better of the Baffin. I am glad now that Duggie has a friend like you. I wasn't always. And you are lucky to have a friend like him because Duggie is the best friend anyone could ever have.

Yours respectfully,
Mara Rydale

Chapter Nine

ON A SUNNY, ROSE-SCENTED DAY IN JUNE, Mara heard the long-awaited sound of coach wheels, glanced out her bedroom window, and went racing down the stairs, shrieking as she passed the kitchen, "Mam, there's a coach outside the door! He must be here!"

Without waiting for Emma, she flung herself through the front door. Sure enough, there was Duggie helping the coachman take down a quantity of luggage.

"Duggie!" she screeched with all the power in her lungs, launching herself at him.

He braced himself to stay on his feet as she showered his face with butterfly kisses and tried at the same time to hug him half to death.

"For God's sakes, let a chap breathe!" said Duggie, getting a firm grip on her waist and lifting her off her feet.

"Oh, Duggie, I missed you so."

"You madcap, I thought you'd be a lady by the time I got home." He capitulated as soon as she looked at him with sorrowful reproach. "I missed you, too, Merry."

At the sound of the pet name only he used for her, Mara renewed her hugging of him. She was in the middle of it when another boy came from around the other side of the coach, dragging a small trunk by its leather handle.

He looked at the girl attached to his friend Duggie like a limpet, at her great laughing black eyes and the wide laughing mouth and the mane of hair thick as a horse's tail, the bluest-blackest hair he had ever seen. She was just as Duggie had described her, just as he had pictured her, full of life and beauty . . . not that Duggie ever used those words, but Roy had made his own interpretation.

Very few things in his life—or even his dream world—had ever lived up to anticipation. He drew a deep breath as Mara let go of Duggie to look at him with frank curiosity.

"Who are you?" she asked in a husky boy-girl sort of voice that sent a queer shiver shooting all through Lord Raleigh Irwine's not-quite-fifteen-year-old body.

"This is my friend Roy," said Duggie with careless ease at the same moment that his friend Roy stepped forward and reached out for one of Mara's hands.

"My lady of the fruitcake," he said solemnly. "I salute you." With the words, he kissed her fingertips, then her thumb.

Mara choked with laughter as she retrieved her hand.

"I told you he was a Bedlamite," said Duggie complacently. Then his expression changed, and his voice. "Mam!" He sprang forward.

Emma held him in her arms. "Oh, my laddie, my laddie."

Mara smiled in happy sympathy even though the "laddie" was taller than his Mam now and he had to bend for her embrace. She looked toward the duke's son, thinking to share this thought with him, and surprised a sudden hungry, almost pained look on his face.

As he caught her eye, the look was gone, and he was himself again, just as she had pictured from Duggie's description, a good-natured, frolicsome boy on the short and stocky—maybe even a bit chubby—side with unruly carroty hair, a face full of freckles, and smiling blue eyes.

"Come meet Mam, Lord Raleigh," Mara said to him.

He frowned a little. "Roy!"

"Oh yes, I forgot," said Mara guiltily. "Lord Roy."

"No, just plain Roy."

Mara shrugged. "It's your name. Whatever

you say." She brought him over to Emma. "Mam, this is Duggie's friend Roy from Eton, and he doesn't want us to use his title."

"He's going to spend the summer at Dumfries Castle, so I told him to come here first, Mam," Duggie put in. "I *told* him you wouldn't mind."

"Indeed and I don't. It's our pleasure to have you, Roy," said Emma warmly as she took his hand. "Why don't you boys carry the bags into the house and come into the kitchen for something to eat while Mara takes the pony to find Da and Donnie. And if you'd like a glass of ale before you leave," she added, turning to the coachman, "stop by at the kitchen too."

"Thanky, ma'am, some ale would set me up fine."

Everyone scattered . . . the coachman and Emma bound for the kitchen, Mara to the stable to get the pony, and Duggie and Roy staggering up the steps of Treeways Cottage with all their luggage.

By the time Mara returned with Angus and Donnie, it was almost lunchtime. Emma and Nurse had spread out a bountiful meal on the trestle table in the kitchen.

The Duke of Ghent's son had never eaten a meal in a kitchen before; he had never partaken of such a merry, noisy family meal with Nurse sitting down to table with her employers as well as her grown nurslings.

He puffed with pride at the casual way

Angus addressed him as "lad" in the same way that he did with Donnie and Duggie. He enjoyed the maternal way the two women pressed food on him. He liked the way Donnie, quickly over his awe of sitting next to a real live lord, whispered to him, "Would you show me that trick of how you lift yourself up in the air and come down somewhere else?"

Roy winked. "Sure. After lunch. Outside."

Most of all he enjoyed watching Mara. Lovely, lively, laughing Mara, with her sparkling eyes and her throaty laugh and her husky boy-girl voice and her exuberant air of well-being. Yes, there was that trick Duggie had mentioned . . . she *did* flick that mane of hair back and forth the way a donkey switched its tail.

Even as he ate a substantial meal, politely answered questions, and contributed to the gaiety of the conversation, his eyes were never far away from Mara.

He smiled secretly as she turned and the hair slapped back and forth along her shoulders; it was as though she were doing it just for his private pleasure.

Then he realized Emma had spoken to him. "I beg your pardon, ma'am. I'm afraid I wasn't attending."

"I only asked if your family would be meeting you at the castle for your holidays."

"I doubt they'll be here this year." Roy shrugged. "My mother prefers to summer near the sea . . . Brighton or Ramsgate. My father's secretary wrote that he would be going on a diplomatic mission abroad. My oldest brother is in Derbyshire, tending my father's chief seat; my brother Oliver is in the navy; and my brother Lucien, the last I heard, was on a visit to the West Indies. My father has properties there."

"You'll be alone all summer at Dumfries?"

"And twenty or thirty servants give or take a dozen," Duggie reminded her.

Emma was looking so troubled that Roy tried to reassure her. "I shall ride and fish and swim and mountain climb, and I'm free to hire any tutors to keep up with my studies." He thought he knew why she still seemed anxious. "I am only planning to inflict myself on you for two days, Mrs. MacTavish."

As he was to mention many times afterward, it was the first time a visit of two days turned into two months.

He rode and fished and swam and climbed, of course, but he did those things in the area of Treeways and with Duggie and Donnie and Mara, and he didn't do them nearly as much as he had expected. He was too busy with the farm chores assigned to him as matter-of-factly by Angus as though Roy were one of his own sons.

When he did a good job of work, he was told so, and when he did a slipshod job, he was told that, too, even more definitely. Without telling, he was expected to correct his mistakes.

Once a week he rode over to Dumfries Castle to collect any mail or messages from the housekeeper and reassure her as to his well-being. One of the MacTavish litter always rode with him because his first joyful act, as soon as his lengthier visit was determined on, had been temporarily to add two fine horses from the castle stables to the modest stable at Treeways.

"Mam." Mara stormed into the kitchen after one such visit when Roy had been with them for about four weeks. "I think the Irwines must be the most horrid family in England."

Emma looked up in surprise from the pie dough she was rolling.

"Did they finally come to the castle?"

"No," said Mara, her cheeks flushed with anger and indignation, "and there wasn't a single letter either. Not *one* in more than a month. And he's been writing to them every week."

"Did he seem to mind?"

"No, he doesn't care. He just made one of his usual silly jokes, but that doesn't make *them* any better, *his* not minding."

Emma gave her a strange look.

"Some people use jokes to cover up hurts, did you ever think on that, lass?"

Mara opened her mouth, then closed it

again. She thought deeply for a moment, with her head cocked to one side. "Then he *does* mind, is that what you're telling me, Mam?" she asked.

"Would you not in his place?" Emma asked quietly.

Slowly Mara shook her head. "No, Mam, I wouldn't mind, not if they weren't worth my minding about."

"It's easy to say, my Mara, when you've never been in his situation."

"But Mam, I *have* been in his situation. My birth mother gave me up to you, and my blood father hardly remembers I'm alive. It doesn't hurt me, truly it doesn't. Whenever I think about it—which isn't often—I am grateful that I got so much the better of the exchange being given over to you and Da."

Their eyes met in love and understanding. Then Emma said, slapping a piece of rolled dough over the first of four pie tins, "But Roy wasn't given any exchange. First it was nurses, then a governess, then school at seven."

"Well, he's got us now," said Mara staunchly.

"Aye, he's got us, but it's not the same, and if you really want to be a friend to him, look behind the jokes sometimes for the sorrow in his heart. It's there."

Mara stood with her head bent for a long moment while Emma began filling her pie tins with sliced apples. Then she fetched a deep sigh and asked, "Can I have a tin to make my own pie, Mam?"

Emma pushed one toward her.

"I'm going out to the orchard to get some peaches," Mara told her, taking a basket down from the shelf. "I'll use your preserved ones if there aren't any left. Roy likes peach pie the best of all."

"Aye," said Emma, eyes twinkling. "It's a short distance from a man's heart to his stomach. Young men or old, food is like love to them."

That night after supper she brought out one of her apple pies for the table and then set the peach pie directly in front of Roy. "Mara fixed this one just for you; she said peach is your favorite."

His eyes lit up. "Any pie you make is my favorite, Mam, but I must admit peach—"

He stopped suddenly, realizing what he had called her. "I beg your pardon, ma'am, I meant no disrespect," he said with the sudden formal dignity that periodically reminded them he *was*, after all, Lord Raleigh Irwine.

Emma said gently, "Nay now, there's not that much difference in sound between Mam and ma'am, and of the two, I must confess I prefer Mam. Happen now, if we're to be so respectful, I'll have to keep it in mind to use your title."

Roy smiled happily. "Don't you dare"—the smile became a grin—"Mam."

Then he lit into the pie. "Did you really make this?" he asked Mara with his mouth full.

"Mam made the crust. I did the filling."

"Marvelous. Could I try a piece of the apple, too?"

Angus chuckled. "That's right, laddie. Learn young that the pretty ones fade, but good cooking lasts forever. Remember that" —he looked at Mara—"when you go off to your fancy school to learn a lot of foolishness."

You're the one who said it would be good for me to learn the foolishness," Mara retorted pertly. "I'd be happier staying right here where I can learn anything I need to know for when Duggie goes in the army and I marry him and follow the drum."

In the stricken silence that followed this proclamation, only Donnie seemed unaffected.

"Are you going to marry Mara?" he asked his brother.

"If she makes up her mind, God help me. I probably won't be given the choice," answered Duggie lightheartedly. "Have you ever known her to make up her mind to something and not get what she goes after?"

Roy pushed back the pie plate, his appetite suddenly gone. His freckles stood out, more prominent than ever, in the sudden whiteness of his face.

Emma looked across the table to Angus, her eyes bleak and her lips trembling.

He tried to send an unspoken message of loving sympathy back to her. *'Twill be all right; she's only a child, love,* his eyes tried to tell her.

But Emma knew full well the moment of truth was here, the day of reckoning had come. Her sin had caught her up.

Chapter Ten

"MARA," ANGUS SAID TO HER AT BREAKFAST the next morning, "I have to go into Carlisle this morning on a business matter. Would you care to ride with me?"

"Of course." Mara sprang up from the table. "I can use a few things from the shops. Do you need anything, Mam?"

Emma shook her head. She seemed tired and worn. Mara looked at her sharply. "Do you have a headache, Mam?"

"A bit of one."

"Maybe I should stay home with you."

"Nay . . . no, I want you to go." Emma spoke so forcefully that Mara jumped in surprise.

"You come with me, lass. Your Mam will be better alone." Angus looked at Emma. "You hear me, woman? Up to your room and to bed."

Emma walked out of the kitchen like a

sleepwalker. They all looked at one another, alarmed, except Angus. "She had a bad night," he said soothingly. "She only needs to catch up on her sleep, then she'll be fine. Out to the barn, lads. Mara, let us be off."

"Mam hardly ever sleeps badly or has a headache," Mara said worriedly when the farm horses attached to the wagon were taking them to Carlisle at a steady trot.

"She was upset because of that talk at the supper table last night about you marrying Duggie. She took it to be serious."

"Doesn't she want me to marry Duggie?" asked Mara, hurt.

"Lassie, she doesn't want you to think of marrying anyone, not before you're even thirteen."

"Oh, I'm not thinking of it for now . . . but later when the school silliness is over for both of us and Duggie's in the army. He'll be lonesome away from the family, and that way my name can be MacTavish and I'll be your true daughter."

"You're my true daughter now, you always will be, lassie; but you have to get it out of your mind that you can marry Duggie. You can't, not ever."

"Is it because I'm a Rydale?"

"It's because," he said gently, "by blood, Duggie is a Rydale too. He's your half-brother, Mara."

"I—I d-don't understand."

"It's a long story, lassie, but I'll try to make

it as short and easy as I can. Maybe you know that your Mam was at Rydale Park as a parlor maid before your parents were married, before she and I even met. I would like to be able to say the whole blame for what happened was your father's, but Emma's always been honest about that . . . she was independent and full of mischief as well as the prettiest thing that ever was, and she says she asked for the trouble she got into with Sir Cuthbert. D'ya *ken* what I'm telling you, Mara?"

"You're saying that—that my father and *Mam . . . they . . . ?*"

"Aye," he said, "but your father was betrothed to your mother, and I had met and fallen in love with Emma . . . and there was a baby on the way."

"The baby was Duggie?"

"Aye."

"You married her knowing? It didn't bother you?"

"It bothered me, but I loved her, and the baby became mine, and Duggie is as much my son as Donnie, just as you are my own daughter to me. But you can understand why talk of marriage between Duggie and you upsets your Mam?"

"So that's why you ran away to Scotland to be married. But why did you never tell us before?"

"Your Mam's afraid and ashamed, lass.

She's mortal feared of losing your love and respect."

"She *never* could."

"I know that, and you do, Mara; you'll have to make sure my Emma knows it too."

Mara smiled cheekily at him. "Aye, Da, I will."

She sat in deep thought for several moments. "I can't get it through my head," she said, "that Duggie's really my own true brother. That's almost better than marrying him," she proclaimed so joyfully that, even as he bit back a smile, Angus knew he could assure Emma in all truthfulness that the love the lass had for their Duggie was not going to ruin either of their lives.

"Does Duggie know?" Mara asked presently.

"Not yet. I decided to speak to you first."

"When are you going to tell him?"

"As soon as we get home from Carlisle. Right now, in fact"—Angus turned his head to smile at her—"if you don't feel a pressing need to get to the shops. I don't have any business in Carlisle that can't wait."

Mara smiled back. "Neither do I."

Angus turned the horses, and Mara gave a little contented wriggle on the wooden seat as they headed back toward Treeways. "You know, Da," she said thoughtfully, "now that we're brother and sister, I could still follow the drum with Duggie and take care of him. It would be perfectly *respectable*."

"It would," said Angus gently, "if people knew—but they mustn't. I want your solemn promise, lass, that you will never tell anyone. You can talk of it with your Mam, with me, with Duggie—but never another person."

"Why not?" wailed Mara. "I *want* people to know that Duggie is my brother."

"Even if it injures him? Even if it hurts your Mam?"

"But why would—?"

"Mara, think, lass. If it became known, there's none would think the worse of *you*, nor even, such is the way of society, of Sir Cuthbert. But my Emma, who holds her head as high as any fine lady in the kingdom, would lose her reputation. And Duggie would be labeled bastard. Unless he's the son of a king or a lord, it's a cruel world out there for a bastard. A mere baronet's illegitimate son would not get very far."

"It's not fair," Mara muttered.

"Life isn't always fair," Angus told her a bit sadly. "That's why I want your promise that you'll never speak of this again to anyone except your Mam or Duggie or me. Not even Donnie. He's a bit straightlaced, our Donnie. I don't want him sitting in judgment on his Mam."

"I give you my word of honor, Da," pledged Mara solemnly. "I will never tell anyone else that Duggie is my real-true brother."

Twenty minutes later she erupted into

Emma's bedroom like a small squall. A quick look showed that the bed was empty; Mam was sitting in the old rocker by the window fast asleep.

Mara tiptoed over to her. The kitchen cat, Mouser, was stretched out on Emma's lap, asleep too. Mam's eyelids were puffy and red. She had been crying. Poor Mam, thought Mara, as she knelt to gently kiss her cheek.

Emma awoke with a start, and the cat, awakened suddenly too, dug his claws into her leg and jumped down from her lap, snarling disapproval.

Mara kissed Emma again, a smackingly exuberant kiss this time. "I've been thinking," she announced, plopping herself down on the floor and hugging her knees. "If Duggie is truly my brother, then that makes *you* more truly my Mam, which is the most wonderful thing that ever was."

Emma looked at this dear foster daughter and started weeping in very un-Emma-like fashion. "I've worrit myself for all these years about what you'd think, and all you have to say is it's wonderful," she sniffed.

"Well," Mara admitted, suddenly a bit shy, "there was *one* thing I wondered about."

"What was that, my Mara?"

"I can understand Sir Cuthbert's wanting —being—well, *liking* you," Mara blurted out awkwardly, "but how could you . . . well, with my *father*, how could you . . . ?"

"It was a long time ago, Mara, so it may be hard for you to believe, but he was a fine figure of a man then. There's more to it than that, though." Emma folded her hands in her lap and looked down into Mara's troubled eyes. "Happen at your age, you can't understand that underneath the cold shell of him, he's very different. He was ever so much a man, Mara, and he made me feel ever so much a woman."

"You really wanted to—to do *that* with him?"

"I really did."

"Were you in love with him?"

"To my shame, no. He just fascinated me."

Mara rocked back and forth on her haunches. "I didn't know you could want to do *that*," she confided, "girls, I mean, without being in love."

"A lot of silliness is talked about how girls feel or are supposed to feel," Emma said, sounding much more like herself. "I wouldn't want you ever to be as foolish as I was, because there's not one man in hundreds would do what my Angus did and not make his woman pay dearly. But that doesn't mean you should be ashamed of the—well, of the sensations in your own body. It's as natural for women as it is for men, for girls as it is for boys, to feel certain . . . urges. The big difference is that a girl has to be ever so much more careful to restrain herself. A man gets honored among his friends for the very act that loses a girl her good name. A man can run away when he's planted the seed and avoid the consequences, but a woman carries the child."

"It's not fair," said Mara for the second time that day.

And Emma, echoing Angus, shrugged as she said lightly, "Life isn't always fair. That's something you had better learn soon as late—along with everything else I've told you."

Mara got the message. "I understand, Mam. And I'll be careful. Anyhow"—her grin was one of pure Mara mischief—"I haven't ever met anyone who made me feel the way you said."

"Praise be that you don't for a good many years!" said Emma tartly. "Where are you off to now?"

"To see Duggie. Da must have told him by now."

She took a few steps back into the room as she saw the shadow cross over Emma's face. "Don't worry about Duggie, Mam. *He* could never think less of you."

Donnie and Roy were together in the stables; she tracked Angus and Duggie down near the cow pasture. They were both leaning against the wooden fence, earnestly talking, and weren't aware of her presence until she flung herself at Duggie.

He staggered under the onslaught of her enthusiastic embrace.

"We're *blood* brother and sister. Isn't it wonderful—except, of course, we can't get married and we can't tell anyone?"

Duggie, who had been looking rather pale and shaken till she appeared, gave Angus a rather shamed, almost shy look across the bent head nuzzling against his shoulder. "Yes," he said, transmitting a message to his "Da" at the same time, "it's wonderful."

Mara straightened up. "Then go speak to Mam and make her comfortable!" she urged him. "She's all in a tizzy now."

Duggie set off for the cottage without another word, just a quick smile for Angus and a quick hug for Mara.

Donnie and Roy strolled over from the stables.

"Don't you ever do anything but kiss and hug lately?" asked Donnie in disgust.

"Well, I guess I can kiss my own two foster brothers if I want to!" Mara declared. She grabbed Donnie and gave him a smack on the forehead.

"Hey, Mara, quit slobbering!" He pulled away from her and turned toward Roy, inviting him to share his repugnance. "Aren't girls the most awful slobberers?"

"Just awful," Roy agreed solemnly.

As though they had both vastly complimented her, Mara curtsied prettily and then went flouncing off. She was surprised, as she reached Emma's flower garden, to find Roy right beside her.

"Aren't you afraid I might slobber over *you*?" The boy-girl voice that was like music to him was full of Mara mischief.

"Not at all!" he retorted promptly. "I was wondering why you never do."

"*You're* not one of my brothers."

"All the more reason." He couldn't help adding sarcastically, "You can't marry both of them."

Mara fetched a deep sigh up from the very depths of her; she might as well, she decided, make a beginning. "Oh, that was just family frolic," she declared. "I'm not going to marry either of them. A girl doesn't marry someone who's been brought up with her like a brother. Why, I'd be more likely to marry . . ." She hunted frantically in her mind for a candidate. "I'd be more likely to marry *you!*" she concluded triumphantly.

The open, freckled face looked strangely shuttered and impassive.

"That is," she added a bit uncertainly, "if a duke's son . . . *could* marry a baronet's daughter."

"This duke's son," said Roy, sounding very much like Lord Raleigh Irwine, "could marry a *farmer's* daughter if he had a mind to."

"My other grandfather is an earl," she mentioned off-handedly.

"Then by all means," said Roy, "let's invite him to the wedding." He grinned, looking again like Roy the prankster. "We're betrothed now; aren't you going to slobber over *me*?"

"I can't."

"Why not?"

"Mam says girls have to be careful because men plant the seeds but *we* get the babies."

Lord Raleigh Irwine flung himself down on the ground and rolled around in mirth. Mara flung herself down beside him on her knees. "Do that gymnick feat," she begged. "The one you did to fool the Baffin."

He obligingly got on his hands and knees, too, levitated, and landed grasshopper-fashion a few feet from her.

"Do it again. Do it again."

This time he landed right beside her, his face very close to hers. "Let's slobber just once," he whispered; then his lips touched hers lightly. Mara found herself leaning forward, suddenly wanting the mouth against hers to press much harder.

"That was lovely," she said sedately as their lips separated. "Did it give you . . . urges?"

"Yes."

"Not me," she said a shade regretfully. "Not the way Mam described. Why do you suppose . . . ?"

"You're less than thirteen," the duke's youngest son explained as kindly and soberly as though he were Angus. Then he tweaked her nose and pinched her bottom, very much

Roy again. "We'll try again in a few years. Save your—er—urges for me."

He grinned as she switched her hair back and forth in her habitual donkey fashion and lifted up her imperious nose and chin. "What I mean," he asked with an exaggerated bow, "is, would you please be so kind, Miss Mara, as to save your urges for me?"

"Very well," said Mara loftily. Then her boy-girl voice got husky and coaxing. "Do the gymnick trick again, please, Roy. *Please*."

Chapter Eleven

Treeways
10th Jan. 18—

Dear Roy,

The day before Christmas your man brought
the sheepdog for Da and the horses for Donnie
and me over from the castle, also the box just
filled to the brim with lengths of silk and lace
trims for Mam and the shawl for Nurse. We
were overwhelmed, and Da was worried about
whether the duke would approve your giving us
such costly gifts; but I told him what you said
in your letter about using your own money
(from your grandmother's inheritance) and
how you *wanted* to . . . and Mam said, "Leave
us not spoil the laddie's joy in giving, Angus."
So then he said all right, and Donnie and I

breathed a sigh of relief because I think we both would have died if we had to give back our horses.

He calls his Beau and I call mine Arrow (Beau and Arrow, are you laughing?) and we ride every day. I use the sidesaddle now, the way my stepmother taught me, because everyone says I will have to when I go away to school.

I am sorry I could only send you the cake and the handkerchiefs and the little sketch of the donkey and me that the traveling artist drew in Carlisle, but I don't have much cash money, though my stepmother explained (when I visited her and Sir Cuthbert during Christmas week) that I will be very rich one day because all my father's money and estate will come to me, as they found out something is wrong with the insides of her, and she can't ever have children. She is very sad because she wanted to give Sir Cuthbert a son; and I thought my father would be very unpleasant about it in the sarcastick way he has of talking (like about my mother not giving him a son), but he was quiet and nice, nicer to me than he ever was and very gentle with Griselda. I think he really likes her.

I wish it were summer again, and you and Duggie could come home to Treeways.

Thank you, thank you for my horse. If you were here, I think I would have to *slobber* over you just one time, I'm so very grateful.

Your friend,
Mara Rydale

P.S. Your letters are great. I'm glad you enjoy mine. Have you been up to any more tricks lately? Duggie says you are getting more serious and you want to go into the army when he does. How come you never told me?

Eton College
3 April 18—

Dear Mara,

I have some perfectly disgusting news. I can't come to Treeways this summer. I had a letter from my father (the first in five years not written by his secretary; I think I'll frame it) telling me that my mother has been quite ill, and though she is recovered now, she needs rest and quiet, so she is spending the summer at Irwine House in Derbyshire, and all the family is bidden to spend the summer there, too. Even the duke will honor us with his presence.

Maybe with luck, toward the end of the summer, I can get to Dumfries for a few weeks . . . but I promise you this, whether I can or I can't come then, I will see you before the end of the year even if I have to get myself expelled to do it.

Thank Mam and Da—thank you for the

latest hamper of sock.* Don't know what we'd do without it. You've saved a score of Etonians from starvation this last year.

> Yr. hmble. obdt. Betrothed,
> Roy Irwine

Several weeks after Duggie's departure for what was to be his last year at Eton, Mara was riding Arrow on her favorite back road parallel to the river Eden when she heard galloping behind her and then the sound of her own name called out.

She turned her head in incredulous joy, unable to believe that it was Roy.

They both came tumbling down from their saddles and ran the short distance that separated them.

Roy lifted her right off the ground. When he set her down on her feet again, "May we slobber just once?" he asked, eyes twinkling.

Mara raised her pursed-up lips and they kissed chastely.

"That was twice," she said accusingly after a minute.

"Well, you said that Mam told you that men aren't to be trusted," Roy returned amiably.

"Man indeed, you oversized Etonian!" she scoffed. Then she took a good look at him. "Good Heavens!" she said. "You really have changed. You're *inches* taller, and you're—

------

*Etonese for "food snacks"

my goodness—you aren't fat anymore," she mentioned frankly, "and the freckles have faded into your skin. Your hair's darker, too, not so red. My stars, you're positively good looking."

Roy laughed self-consciously, more pleased than he would ever have been willing to admit. "I wish I could return the compliment and call *you* good looking," he said.

"Can't you?" asked Mara, rather chagrined, tossing her mane of blue-black hair over her shoulders in the way he never tired of seeing.

"No," said Roy, itching to get hold of the mane and rub its soap-scented thickness over his face. "You're not good looking, Mara Rydale, you're beautiful."

Mara threw herself into his arms. "Oh, you darling, to say it!" she caroled joyously. "Sometimes I've wondered . . . you know . . . when I look into my mirror, but Nurse always says, Beauty is as beauty does, and Mam says it's from within, and Da says it doesn't mean as much as character. Duggie tells me I look like a gypsy and Donnie thinks the new prize hog is prettier than me. It's all a bit discouraging."

She looked up into the dear familiar face, changed only enough to make him seem—well, almost handsome.

"Have I really grown beautiful too?" she asked.

"No," said Roy. "You always *were* beautiful, both inside and out."

She promptly stood on tiptoe to kiss him again. Then they tied their horses to trees and sat down on the banks of the river to talk.

"How was Derbyshire this summer?"

Roy shrugged. "Grim. My mother is recovering but delicate. Loud sounds—like my voice—offend her nerves. A fifteen-minute visit a day sufficed. My father and older brother were fairly busy about the estate. My brother Oliver was home part of the summer on leave, and he smuggled his London mistress to a small lodge lying empty on the estate and incarcerated the poor girl there so he could visit her at his ease. Lucien was busy studying most of the time. He plans to take orders soon, thank God."

"Why thank God?" asked Mara even as she reached for his hand to press his fingers sympathetically.

"Because the oldest son inherits the estates, of course. The younger ones, according to how many there are, divide the spoils the family can provide in the army, navy, and church. My father had always intended the church for me. Two handsome livings were saved and I was expected to rise from them to bishop, disinclination notwithstanding." He shrugged. "Now that Lucien has chosen the church, there will be no objections to my going into the army."

"And what," Mara inquired with a pretense of severity, "are you doing *here* when you should be at Eton . . . or daren't I ask?"

He grinned engagingly. "Eton—that is to say, the Baffin decided that my enlivening presence at that hallowed hall of learning could be dispensed with."

"And how," asked Mara accusingly, "did you get him to decide that?"

"Fairly easily," said Roy. "I challenged him to a duel, and on his declining, I—er—borrowed a small cannon from a group of soldiery and fired it underneath the Baffin's window, while reissuing my challenge."

"You *are* a Bedlamite!" Mara shook her head, half admiring, half perturbed. "Expulsion for a silly lark . . . I thought you had finally grown up. What did the duke say?"

"I didn't stay to find out," answered Roy disarmingly. "I was fortunately in funds at the time, so I took off by chaise for the castle. When he eventually gets the letter from Dr. Keate, he will no doubt have his secretary write to express his displeasure. And it wasn't a silly lark. It was deliberate. I wanted to be expelled."

"Wanted to!" said Mara, scandalized. "But why?"

Roy eyed her steadily, and she turned a bright scarlet.

"You couldn't . . . you didn't . . . ."

"Silly lark, that's what you really think, isn't it?" he exploded. "By God, I'm seventeen and I have been at Eton since the age of seven. Ten years is enough. More than enough. I'm going to stay at the castle for a bit, and when my father wants to know what I intend to do with my life, I'll ask him to purchase my commission. Or maybe you think," he asked bitterly, "an eleventh year of Greek and Latin would serve me better?"

"No. What I think," Mara said soothingly, taking both his hands, "is that you should stay at Treeways with us, not alone at the castle."

"I can't," Roy answered quietly, "not when I'm here without his Grace's consent and have taken French leave of Eton before the Baffin got a chance to write to my father. I've already spoken to Mam and Da about it; that's how I knew where to find you. If my father, the duke, gets on his high horse about what I've done, I don't want any of the MacTavishes to be involved in his displeasure. It won't be too different from our last summer. I'll just sleep at the castle and visit as often as I can."

He stood up and reached down to pull her to her feet. "Let's go home to Treeways," he said. "I've been invited for lunch."

Chapter Twelve

MARA CAME HOME FROM HER FAVORITE RIDE along the river Eden one Sunday morning, disappointed that Roy had not met her along the way as he so often did. She was not especially overjoyed to find Sir Cuthbert Rydale's elegant paneled carriage standing in front of the cottage waiting for her.

The coachman, Gardner, was on the box and touched his hat to her.

"Mistress MacTavish have a message for 'ee, Miss Mara," he told her.

Emma had the message in its sealed envelope in her apron pocket. She produced it the moment Mara dashed into the kitchen and watched worriedly while her foster daughter slit open the envelope with a small kitchen knife and read the four lines over the signature, Cuthbert Rydale, Bt.

"Oh, damn!" said Mara aloud.

"Mara!"

"Sorry, Mam, but it *is* provoking. Why does he have to decide I should visit Rydale just when Roy is here? And he says he wants to discuss my schooling. I don't like the sound of that."

"You've known for years he intended to send you to school."

"Yes, but I hoped I could put it off for another year," Mara said frankly, then frowned a little. "I don't like the sound of *this*"—she indicated her father's letter—"*the time has come.*"

Emma sighed, not liking the sound of it either but not wanting to encourage Mara in an attitude of rebellion that would do her no good.

"A very methodical man he is, your father. Happen he's just planning for the future," she said with forced cheerfulness. "Come, let's pack your portmanteau. The sooner you go, the sooner you return."

Sir Cuthbert's plans for his daughter were not as immediate as Mara had feared, but they *were* quite definite.

Their private session in the library after dinner that night—Griselda having tactfully excused herself from joining them with a murmured excuse of some letters to write—went on more promisingly than it began.

After studying his daughter from across his desk for a few moments, as though he had never seen her before, "You will be the only one to carry on the Rydale blood," he said, "since I can no longer expect to have a son."

"Except Duggie," Mara reminded him with a sweet smile.

"Douglas *MacTavish*"—Sir Cuthbert emphasized the surname—"has been amply provided for. Nor do I see any reason," he added in some annoyance, "why Emma should have told you of his circumstances. Had I wanted you to know them, then I—"

"*Mr.* and *Mrs.* MacTavish," Mara interrupted, emphasizing as deliberately as he had, "judged it best I be told the truth when I began to talk about marrying Duggie."

"*Marry* Duggie!" Sir Cuthbert gave a strangled cough into a fine linen handkerchief, then emerged from it, his face very red, to say firmly, "Nonsense. When the time comes, I will choose a husband for you . . . preferably—I intend to look about among the Rydale connections . . . but there is no great hurry."

"Of course not," said Mara, greatly relieved. "No great hurry at all. I'm not even fifteen."

In our prize hog's eye, you will choose my husband! she said to herself but wisely didn't repeat the thought out loud.

"Still, you must soon be educated to take your place in the world of fashion," Sir Cuthbert went on in his pompous way. "And though Emma MacTavish is a very good sort of woman," he informed Emma's foster daughter condescendingly, "she is hardly fit to prepare you to lead the kind of life that will be yours hereafter."

Mara folded her hands in her lap to keep them from clenching into fists. She even managed a tight smile.

"Have you decided on my school?" she asked. "Is it close by?"

"Your stepmother attended a seminary in Bath, where she thinks you would be happy. It has a greater degree of freedom than most schools, she tells me, and less rigidity of attitude. There are also stabling arrangements so that you would be able to ride regularly. I am sure that would be as important to you as it was to Griselda."

"Yes," said Mara in some relief, "I don't want to give up riding."

"I have been in correspondence with the headmistress, Miss Petersham. She is ready to receive you by the end of the month."

"The end of the month—oh, no!" Mara cried out.

"There is some impediment?" her father inquired courteously.

"It's a b-bit t-too s-soon. I would rather wait until next September. "I'm—I'm not quite ready to leave ho—Treeways yet."

"You will have to make the break with Treeways sooner or later, Mara," Sir Cuthbert told her firmly but not unkindly. "Let us compromise. Shall we say in six months' time? You could attend the spring semester, which would mean only a few months of school before you returned to Cumberland for the summer. That should make your accommodation to the change more easy. Moreover, I would allow you to spend one last summer at Treeways. Thereafter, though you will be free to visit there, of course, you will have to make your home here at Rydale with Griselda and me, so you will become accustomed to the way you must go on. One day Rydale will be yours."

Mara was quick-witted enough to understand that, according to his own code, Sir Cuthbert was dealing with her generously. If she acted unwisely, she might lose the little she felt she had gained.

"Thank you, sir," she forced herself to say, then stood up and curtsied deeply in order to show him that Emma had not been as lacking in the instruction of manners as he seemed to think. "May I be excused, sir? I should like to speak to Griselda about her school."

"Yes, certainly," said Sir Cuthbert. "An excellent notion. You will probably find her in the small sitting room the other side of the breakfast parlor."

Mara curtsied again and backed out of the library, closing the door. She walked right past the small sitting room and dashed upstairs to her bedroom.

Griselda found her lying on her back on the bed an hour later. A quick look told her that her stepdaughter had not been crying; she looked stormy-eyed and defiant rather than tearful.

Griselda sat down on the side of the bed. "I know how you feel, Mara, truly I do. I didn't want to go to school either, and though I had the kindest parents in the world, they insisted, knowing it was for my own good. They didn't want me to hide away from life forever in the shelter of my family."

"I'm not afraid of life, if that's what you mean!" Mara denied.

"Not of life itself, perhaps, in the way that I was," said Griselda thoughtfully, "but of life outside Treeways, the life of the future mistress of Rydale that you were born to but not bred to—I think you are afraid of that."

She pressed Mara's hand comfortingly. "I know it's not your fault, and I thank you for not reminding your father that he, not you, was responsible for having you reared away from Rydale. But I really think you may enjoy Miss Petersham's. Much to my surprise, when I got there, I did. She's a rather extraordinary woman who believes women are more than animated dolls dressed and trained for snaring husbands. She believes that they—*we*—should develop our own interests and talents so that in case of need, we can take care of ourselves."

She laughed a little ruefully. "You must not judge the other pupils by me," she told Mara. "One of the girls who was my close friend went to Italy to study painting; one became a professional singer. Several got good teaching positions. Even among those who married, there is one that contributes articles to literary magazines in London."

"Since I have to go, whether I want to or not," said Mara at her most sensible, "then I'm glad you chose a place like Miss Petersham's. It doesn't sound as awful as I expected. And Sir Cuthbert said I could ride as often as I wanted. Is that true?"

"Oh yes, I rode three or four times a week, whenever weather permitted. There's a special groom attached to the stables where Miss Petersham's pupils rent their horses. He takes out groups of two or three girls at a time."

"Thank you, Griselda. I appreciate your talking to my father."

"Not at all, dear. I wrote to Miss Petersham about your classics studies with Mr. Newcastle. I assure you she is quite looking forward to having such a highly qualified pupil."

Chapter Thirteen

THE DAY BEFORE MARA WAS DUE TO GO BACK to Treeways cottage her stepmother received an express from London summoning her to her mother's sickbed. Maids were set to hasty packing and within two hours Griselda was on her way, accompanied by Sir Cuthbert.

Mara, helped by one of the maids, was attending to her own packing when a footman came up to ask if she would receive Lord Raleigh Irwine.

She slammed shut the lid on her smaller portmanteau, instructed the maid, "Just throw everything else into the big one," and raced for the stairway.

Remembering when she arrived at the head of the stairs that her rigidly formal father was not in residence, Mara gave in to a wish she had cherished since her first visit at age six. She tucked her skirts about her

legs and went sliding down the carved wood-
en balustrade. *Un*luckily for her, it was so
curved and so steep that she gathered too
much momentum and flew off when she
reached the end. *Luckily* for her, her visitor
had waited below in the hallway and, by
barreling into him, she broke her fall.

"As you quite recently said to me," Lord
Raleigh Irwine mentioned a bit breathlessly
from his prone position alongside her on the
marble hallway floor, "I thought you had
finally grown up."

But his eyes were dancing with enjoyment
as he got up on one knee and stretched out
both hands to pull her to her feet. Mara
laughed, accepted his hands, and the two of
them got up together.

"How did you know?" she asked, brushing
off her skirts.

"Know what?"

"That I was coming home ahead of time."

"I didn't. I came direct from the castle. I
thought perhaps you might be allowed to go
for a ride with me. Cook prepared a picnic
lunch. Are you in a hurry to get back to
Treeways?"

"No, and a picnic lunch sounds wonderful
to me. Everything's been so proper here. I'll
just change to my riding habit before it gets
packed. Want to wait in the library?"

"No, I'll walk around to the stables."

"Good. You can order Jojo to be saddled for
me when you get there."

When Mara came downstairs again, stepping sedately this time, she wore the new if slightly crushed midnight-blue riding dress that Griselda had just given her, as well as a matching bonnet with a dyed blue feather.

"Handley," she told the aged butler, "would you please have two of the grooms bring my bags to Treeways tomorrow morning. Then one of them can ride Jojo back."

Since her father was not present to object to this breach of protocol, she added, "Thank you for all your kind care, Handley," and curtsied as deeply to him—to his pleased shock—as she did to Sir Cuthbert.

Roy raised one eyebrow when he saw the smart new riding habit and both eyebrows at the sight of a bonnet covering the thick blue-black hair.

"A present from Griselda," Mara explained. As soon as they were out of sight of the stables, she pulled off the bonnet and tied it to Jojo's saddle.

"There!" she said with satisfaction and the usual toss of her head, swishing her hair. "I feel more like myself."

"You look more like yourself too," said Roy, watching the mane of hair switch back and forth as they cantered. "But that shade of blue becomes you."

"Thank you kindly, sir."

"You are welcome, ma'am. Where do you want to go? The river road? Carlisle Castle? Something new?"

"How about Hardknott Castle near Ambleside? Duggie and I always talked of tackling that mountain road, but we somehow never did."

"Is it tricky?"

"It's a bit of a climb, I've heard."

"What's so special about Hardknott?"

"Well, it's not so much a castle as an old Roman fort," said Mara slyly, knowing Roy shared Duggie's passion for military history. "It would be fun to have our picnic there, and we do have half the morning and the whole of the afternoon."

It was an unseasonably warm day for October, and they were both hot and hungry by the time they got to Ambleside. They stopped at a small shepherd's hut for directions, then went on just a short distance till they came to a clearing that was shaded by tall trees and had a stream meandering through it.

They watered the horses in the stream and fed them carrots and lumps of sugar from Roy's knapsack of provisions. Both decided it would be a good idea to eat in this comfortable spot before going on, so Roy spread one of the saddle blankets for them to sit on. Then he shook out a Scottish wool plaid he always carried to use as a serving cloth.

"Don't say it!" he warned, noticing Mara silently convulsed with laughter and about to speak.

"Say what?" she asked, opening her eyes wide at him.

"What you were about to say."

"How can you possibly know what *I* was about to say?"

"In the time-honored words of the Baffin, 'I see guilt in your eye.'"

"Well," she said in tones of injured innocence, "I think you're doing me a great injustice to assume I was going to mention that you resembled Sir Walter Raleigh spreading out his c—"

He made a grab for her, squeezing her waist so hard she didn't have the breath to finish. "You," he told her severely, "are about to get your ears soundly boxed—unless you're willing to pay a forfeit."

"What's the forfeit?"

"Guess?" said Roy, and pressed his mouth to hers.

Presently Mara's arms wrapped around his neck and his around her back. It was a long, long time before he lifted his head. When he finally did, Mara looked up wonderingly into his bright blue, strangely serious eyes.

"Gracious goodness!" she said. "I feel . . . peculiar."

"Urges?" he asked lightly.

"I'm not sure. I do . . . rather . . . tingle."

"Urges." Roy nodded his head, vastly pleased.

"If you say so," Mara murmured. "Shall we try again?"

"No," said Roy. "I think perhaps we had better eat."

"Whatever you say." A bit disappointed but compliant, she flopped down onto the blanket and Roy started to unwrap some of the neat little paper-wrapped parcels.

"Sandwiches of chicken, cheese, and ham . . . take your pick. Let me see, I think the pickles are in here."

"Did your cook think you were proposing to feed half the British Army?" asked Mara, chomping on a pickle.

"She knows I'm a growing boy," said Roy complacently as he helped himself to one of each kind of sandwich. "Oh, this jar is lemonade for you and this one ale for me. You may have my silver cup . . . I'll drink from the jar."

"What a gentleman you are, my lord," said Mara, accepting the cup.

"What a minx you are!" retorted Roy, pouring out her lemonade.

When they ended their lunch with some of the special Dumfries Castle pastries and a plum and nectarine each, even Roy confessed for once to being full to bursting. They packed a good half of their picnic lunch and returned it to Roy's knapsack, then proceeded on their way, arriving in a few minutes of hard riding at the beginning of the steep, narrow climb to Hardknott.

"Good Lord, we'll have to leave the horses below," Roy said. "Maybe we shouldn't attempt going up today. It looks fairly rugged, and it's a bit later in the day than I planned we'd begin."

"Oh, come on, don't be chicken-hearted," Mara urged him lightheartedly as she slid down from Jojo and tied the reins around a tree. Roy shrugged and did the same.

"Take your hat," he advised. "We'll be out in the sun a good part of the way."

Mara nodded and untied the bonnet from her saddle and jammed it carelessly onto her head, leaving the ribbons loose.

Roy threw the plaid across his shoulder. "We may want something to sit on up there. Shall I take the lemonade?"

"I wouldn't bother," said Mara carelessly. "There's usually a little water along these mountain rocks."

They climbed side by side for a long while, with so little room to spare it seemed quite natural for Roy to take her hand and bring them together even closer.

Presently the path became more narrow; they had to separate and walk single file.

"Stay close behind me!" he told her sharply. "Hold on to my jacket if you want."

As they went forward again, with Mara close behind him but *not* holding on to his jacket, he tossed a belligerent ultimatum back to her. "If this doesn't improve soon, we're turning back. Some things can be *too* adventurous."

"It is the cowish terror of his spirit/That

dares not undertake," retorted Mara sweetly. "Shakespeare . . . *King Lear*. A fine soldier you'll make."

Roy stopped short, causing her to bump into him. "*Wrens make prey where eagles dare not perch.* . . . also Shakespeare . . . more succinctly put by Alexander Pope. *Fools rush in where angels fear to tread.* Survival, for your information, my heedless one, happens to be one of the primary obligations of a soldier."

They went on in silence for another five or six minutes, Roy saving his breath for climbing and Mara temporarily bereft of a smart answer.

He had just begun, "I really think—" and Mara, in her heart, was inclined to agree with what he *really* thought, when the path all at once took a curling turn around a soaring rock pile and widened so considerably that, over a long rock slab to the side, someone had built an arborlike shelter of vines and tree branches. Covered with earth and twigs, like a great arching bird's nest, this shady-looking and very welcome haven was obviously meant to serve as a resting spot.

"This is more like it," Roy enthused.

"Let's rest a bit," Mara suggested.

"We'll rest a bit," Roy agreed, "before we turn back. No," he added as Mara tried to speak, "that's not an opinion or a question, it's a statement of fact. We are *not* going on. If you want to try it again one day, we'll start out much earlier, wearing sensible walking shoes."

"I wasn't going to argue," said Mara with unwonted meekness, limping toward the slab and sliding down to the ground with her back to it. "My feet do hurt a bit." She started pulling off her boots.

"You really *are* a fool," said Roy in a scoldingly fond voice as he knelt at her feet to help her. "Where does it hurt?"

She indicated her left heel, and he felt it gently through her stocking. "I think you may have a blister forming."

"I know I do."

He shook his head. "God, you are the stubbornest thing in nature!"

"Duggie says it's not sporting to hit a man when he's down," said Mara reproachfully.

"Duggie is right." He slid down alongside her, pulled her legs matter-of-factly across his lap, and gently stroked the aching feet.

"That feels lovely," sighed Mara. "Wake me up when it's time to go." She closed her eyes.

Roy closed his eyes, too, meaning it to be for just a minute. When he opened them again, he was cramped and chilled and the world seemed to be made of gray nothingness, day and night intermingled. The only reality was Mara's legs across his lap and

Mara's body—he felt for it—propped against the rock slab.

He sat very quiet, not wanting to disturb her, but he already had.

Her usually throaty voice sounded shrill in the eerie, silent spacelessness, a little tentative, a lot frightened. "Roy, what's happened?"

In the need to reassure her, he immediately had command of himself again. "Nothing unusual, except for my stupidity in letting us get caught up in it. We're fogged in."

"You're not God, you know; *you* can't take credit for making fog."

Roy chuckled.

"Pray what do you find so humorous in this situation?"

"You." He continued to chuckle. "You are my never-ending source of delight, Mistress Mara Rydale. You can always depress my pretensions by being never-failingly tarter than a gooseberry pie."

"And that amuses you?"

"Amuses and entrances."

"Goody for you," said Mara, suddenly forlorn. "I find it scary."

"Give me your hand."

Mara began to giggle a little hysterically. "What now?"

"I'm holding my own hand out, but I can't see it."

"Neither can I. Stay still."

Presently his groping hand found hers, squeezing it comfortingly.

"What time do you suppose it is?" asked Mara.

"I haven't a notion. Late afternoon, early evening—it could be either."

"Are we stuck up here for the night?"

"I'm afraid so."

"Will the horses be all right?"

"Probably a lot more comfortable than we are."

"At least no one will worry about us," Mara reassured herself and him. "Mam and Da think I'm at Rydale, and at Rydale they think I've gone home to Treeways."

"And at Dumfries they'll think I stayed over at the cottage."

"So everything's fine," said Mara, teeth chattering, "except that I'm c-c-cold."

Roy swore, then remembered he had brought his plaid with him. "Feel around on the ground for my Scots plaid. It's wool."

They both started scrabbling their hands on the earth floor for a few minutes. "Got it!" said Roy triumphantly. "Now take your legs away and turn your back to me."

Mara obeyed a bit slowly and reluctantly, only to have his hands return to her waist and lift her onto his lap.

"Lean against me" was the next gruff command.

She leaned very gladly, and the big wool

plaid was wrapped around her, then tucked in underneath her. "How do you feel now?" he whispered, his mouth close to one ear.

"Snug as a baby . . . in her big brother's arms," mumbled Mara, snuggling closer.

A stiffening of the legs under her and the arms around her, an ominously hostile silence, made her aware that she might have said the wrong thing.

"*I* am *not* your *brother*," said Lord Raleigh Irwine, pulling up his legs and tumbling her tight against his chest. "Permit me to prove it."

Chapter Fourteen

"Kissing and hugging," said Mara sometime later, "is a very warming exercise."

"Actually," murmured Roy, roping her long mane of hair around his wrist, "I'm rather hot myself."

"I wouldn't call it hot," Mara pronounced judiciously. "I'm just comfortable." She wriggled a little on his lap. "Are you *sure* I'm not too heavy for you?"

"We've already discussed that. Stay right where you are."

She leaned back against him. "I'll be pleased to if you insist."

"I insist."

"Good." She yawned. "Have you kissed a lot of girls, Roy?"

"Why?" he grunted.

"You do it so well, I thought perhaps you must have."

"How would *you* know? Have you been kissed by so many boys?"

"You're the first," she told him cheerfully.

"Well, I can't claim the same. There were a couple of housemaids who worked for my dame at Eton . . . my cousin Edith in London. Oh yes, a dairy maid in Derbyshire and Lady Jean Hartley's daughter at Dumfries Castle a few years ago. Not to mention a strumpet my father introduced me to this past summer."

"Why in the world did he do that?" asked Mara, sitting up straight to peer at him, forgetting she couldn't see a thing. She felt Roy's shrug.

"Having allowed Eton to handle my education for these ten or eleven years, he decided to crowd as much fatherly instruction as he could into a couple of months. It consisted, for the most part, of telling me all that was wrong with me, much of which I already knew. I am aware that my three brothers are tall, lean, handsome, and fair-haired, and that I am shorter, stockier, far from handsome, and unaccountably redheaded."

Mara said indignantly, "You are *splendid* looking." Her kiss missed the intended target of his mouth and landed on his nose.

She felt him relax a little. His laugh sounded genuinely amused. "I told his Grace, any complaints of that nature should be addressed to my mother, not to me. He did not appreciate my humor, but he dropped the subject and went on to my academic achievements or lack of them. Dr. Keate, it seems, had told him I had a superior brain, but what was the use of having one, he wanted to know, if I never used it. I promised to try to do so in the future, and he was so appeased that he waxed quite paternal and offered to make a man of me. That's when he took me to a—er—House of Higher Education and introduced me to the strumpet."

"Did you like it?"

"Like what?"

"You know . . . being with a . . . with a whore."

"I'm afraid I didn't get to find out."

Suddenly she could see his face, very dim, very pale, rather disembodied. "The fog's lifting a little," Mara said happily. "I can see you a bit. Can you see me?"

"Yes."

"What are we going to do? Should we try to go down?"

"No, we're going to stay right where we are till morning. The dark is as treacherous as the fog up here. One wrong step and we could tumble over the mountain."

Mara returned to the matter of the strumpet.

"Why didn't you get to find out?" she asked urgently.

She saw his mouth constrict, and then the fog came back, swirling around his face again, but the three agonized words came loud and clear through the mist. "I—couldn't —perform."

"I don't understand."

"Neither do I!" Roy cried in anguish. "She was willing. She took me into her bed, and God knows I've been wanting—but I couldn't —I—and my father knows. My father, God damn!" She could hear his fist pounding against the ground. "He wanted to know afterward if I'd been corrupted at Eton . . . did I like boys?"

Mara slid off his lap, her heart aching with pity and pain for him. She knelt in front of him, gathering him into her arms, rocking him and loving him.

"I hate him for hurting you like this!" she whispered fiercely.

"But he did—quite rightly—make me wonder about myself. Something has to be wrong with me. Why *couldn't* I when I've been wanting a woman . . . I *thought* I wanted a woman for ages?"

"Did—did you like her?"

"She was a nice enough woman, I suppose," he muttered. "Too much paint on her face for my taste, and her perfume was so strong it gagged me when she got close and—"

"And?"

"Well, you know, started—taking off my clothes."

"Did you kiss her the way you kissed me?"

"Not after we got into bed. God!" He

pounded the ground again. "I've got no business to be talking to you like this."

"Yes, you do. We're friends, and I want to know. Why didn't you kiss her anymore in bed?"

"I just didn't want to. The whole thing repelled me."

"Would it repel you to kiss *me* if *I* had no clothes on?"

"Don't be—Mara, stop it!"

"Do you want *me*, Roy?"

The only sound in the night was his ragged breathing.

"If you don't, just say so, and I won't bother you anymore."

"Oh, sweet Jesus, Mara, you know I want you."

"Then show me what to do. Make love to me, please."

With Mara still on his lap, he bent over to spread the plaid on the ground; then he lifted her onto it and slid down beside her.

"Lie on your side, facing me," he whispered.

Mara turned round. With her fingers, she lightly outlined his face. "I wish I could see you," she whispered back.

"I'm here, sweetheart." Roy laughed shakily. "I'm very solid, very real. See?"

He kissed her so thoroughly she felt warm all over, despite the chill wind blowing through their arbor against her unprotected back. But when Roy's arms went around her, he felt the wind, and he made her switch positions with him so that the rock slab sheltered her on one side, his body on the other.

"Am I supposed . . . shall I take off my clothes?" Mara asked him presently, when there was a pause in the kissing and his searching hands were still.

He laughed again, happily amused.

"I don't think that would be a good idea, Mistress Mara. I don't want a frozen maid in my arms."

"But how . . . ?"

"We'll manage . . . trust me. We'll manage . . . somehow."

He unbuttoned her jacket, his fingers a bit stiff and awkward until they found the treasure beneath her chemise. Then they moved all over her with such instinctive soft sensitivity that Mara could only lie there, silently enraptured.

Presently she gave a little shiver, and Roy, misinterpreting, thought that she was cold. He buttoned her jacket swiftly, and she was too ashamed to cry out the wanton wish in her heart. *Oh no, don't stop, don't stop!*

He had no intention of stopping, but the next exploration took place beneath her petticoats. This time, though she still didn't speak, he understood the quivering response of her body and exulted in each spasmodic reaction to his loving, unpracticed motions.

Mara was roused from her ecstasy by the

sounds he was making. "Are you in pain?" she asked, alarmed.

In response to this artless question, he gave a spurt of laughter, then began to choke. "Quite dreadful p-pain," he managed to gasp out.

Mara started to sit up. "What shall we do?" He pushed her back down again.

"We're doing it, my precious idiot! The cure for my pain is *you*."

"Oh!" said Mara, relieved and happy. "Go ahead then."

She tugged up her skirt and petticoats while he took off his jacket and swung himself over her, his palms flat on the plaid alongside her shoulders. She unconsciously braced herself to take his weight, but still he hesitated.

"Mara, it's not too late. I can still . . . Are you *sure*?"

"For pity's sakes, yes, I'm sure."

"I'm sorry," said his muffled voice into her shoulder not too many minutes later. "I tried not to hurt you, but I know I was clumsy."

"You were *not* clumsy," Mara contradicted him as she caressed the back of his head and neck. "You were very—" She hunted in her mind for the proper word and came up with, "Gentlemanly. Mam told me the first time almost always hurts a little for a girl," she added matter-of-factly. "Does it for a man, too?"

"I can't speak for other men, only myself.

If it did, it was a hurt I'd gladly have again and again."

He pulled down her skirts and lay beside her on the plaid, gathering her into his arms.

"Thank you for the wonderful gift you gave me, Mara Rydale." He spoke against her hair. "I don't think I have ever in my life been quite so happy as at this moment."

"You're very welcome." Mara snuggled closer. "I feel good too."

"They'll have to rewrite the Bible."

"Wh—why?"

"You know. *They could not drink of the waters of Marah, for they were bitter.* Exodus. *I* drank of the waters of Mara"—his arms tightened convulsively—"and they were incredibly sweet."

Mara moved a few inches back from him so she could get one hand inside his shirt and dance it across his chest, pausing now and then to curl a tendril of hair around one of her fingers.

"You mustn't think I was just being noble," she told him earnestly. "You were right, I think." Her hand moved around to his back. "I did feel *urges*. Tell me, how often do you think one feels them?"

"If you keep on doing the kind of things you are doing to me, probably all the time."

"You mean . . . ?"

"I'm afraid so."

"Why afraid?"

"Well—"

"I feel them too. Perhaps"—she took her hand from inside his shirt and touched it tentatively to his cheek—"perhaps we could take longer this time, and it would be . . . I don't know . . . it just seemed to end too soon."

The words were hardly out of her mouth before he was kissing her again, crushing her with his body, swearing at the clothes that got in his way, holding her as though he would never let her go, and, finally, when she knew she would die if he waited another minute, he loved her for a much longer time.

Chapter Fifteen

THE FOG HAD ALL BUT LIFTED; THERE WAS even a sliver of moonlight. They could see each other dimly.

"I hate myself!" said Mara suddenly, and Roy raised himself up on one elbow to look down at her in panic.

She was sorry, he told himself, his heart descending sickly to his stomach. "Why?" he asked her, afraid to hear the answer.

"For not saying yes when you asked if you should bring the lemonade," wailed Mara. "I'm a little thirsty and a lot hungry."

He hugged her hard in his relief. "Is that all?"

"*All*? When I tell you I'm starving?" said Mara indignantly.

"Do you think I would let you starve, my little one?"

"I don't see that you have much choice, stuck up on this mountain." She looked up at their arbor. "Unfortunately, these vines and branches don't bear fruit."

"But others do," said Roy mysteriously, crawling about on all fours and peering into the darkness. "Where the devil did I throw my jacket? Oh, there it is."

He sat down on the plaid again, holding his jacket in the air. "I foolishly listened to you about the lemonade, dear girl," he said, digging into one jacket pocket. "But otherwise I was my usual provident self. Behold."

He tossed two small paper-wrapped parcels onto her lap. "Two somewhat squashed but still edible chicken sandwiches. Not a feast, perhaps, but they'll keep starvation at bay. And in here"—he was exploring the other pocket and rolled the contents at her feet—"peaches. One, two, three. They'll somewhat help the thirst."

Mara flung herself at him. "You're wonderful."

"Hey, don't mash the fruit."

But when they were seated side by side on the plaid again, leaning against the rock slab, each eating a sandwich and peach, eating slowly, trying to make them last, his eyes twinkled in the old familiar way. Laughter sounded in his voice even as he pretended to melancholy.

"It's a bit daunting that you were much more complimentary about my prowess in producing peaches and sandwiches than—er —other feats."

"Who said I was?"

"Your own words. I didn't hear any *'You're wonderful'* coming from you *before* I provided the food."

"You were wonderful," said Mara, *"before* you provided food."

He couldn't speak for the lump in his throat or tease for the joy in his heart. He pulled her onto his lap again and nuzzled his face against her. She thought she felt the damp of tears on her neck but tactful, for once, refrained from mentioning it.

Instead, "How shall we divide the peach?" she asked practically, picking the last one up from the plaid. "You eat half, then I'll eat half, or should we each take one bite by turns?"

"The last peach is all for you," said Roy.

"No, that's not fair. We share *equally*," said Mara, her lips stubbornly set as she laid the peach down.

Roy tumbled her off his lap onto the plaid and stood up to put on his jacket. When he had buttoned the last silver button, he suddenly went down on one knee and, picking up the peach, held it out to her.

"It was the custom in ancient times," he said softly, "for a lord or knight to give his lady a first-day gift in return for the great gift she had given him in the night. My lady Mara, this peach is my gift to you."

It was important to him that she take the peach. Mara felt a sudden rush of tears to her own eyes; she didn't exactly know why, except that there was something strange and beautiful about the night and the moment and the sliver of moon that showed Roy, no clown now, seeming to stand tall against the mountain even as he half knelt to her, holding out the peach.

She took the peach. "Thank you for your lovely gift, m-m-my lord," she gulped.

He never changed his position while she ate every bit of it, then wiped her mouth with the paper wrapping from her sandwich.

"It was delicious," she said, unaccountably shy, less willing to meet his steady gaze now than before.

When he said, sounding quite normal, "I think we should try to get some sleep now, Mara; it's still a long night ahead," she felt a sudden release of tension.

"Yes," she said, lying obediently on the plaid. "I am rather tired."

"I, too," said Roy, the laughter in his voice again. He lay beside her, and his arms went around her in the most natural way. Her curves seemed to fit so comfortably and so exactly into his. "Like we were made to be that way," she murmured.

"What did you say?"

He couldn't see her blush in the pale bit of moonlight. "Oh, nothing." She waited till he was half dozing to say his name urgently. "Roy."

"Huh?"

"When you get back to the castle tomorrow, you know what I want you to do first thing?"

"Hmm?"

"Write a letter to your father. Is he still in Derbyshire?"

Roy came awake in a hurry. "No, in London. Why do you want me to write to him?"

"So you can tell him that you *weren't* corrupted at Eton and—and you perform *admirably* with someone you like and who likes you . . . and *you* don't have to pay a strumpet."

His great roaring shout of laughter echoed back and forth across the mountain as he seized her and pulled her on top of him. "Mara, sweet waters of Mara, I shall write my letter before I eat or bathe or change my clothes, and I shall send it to London express."

He switched his grip on her wrists to an arm-hold around her waist and rolled over, cradling her as they reversed positions.

"I'm suddenly not sleepy at all," Roy declared, "nor even very tired. How about you?"

"Well, I . . . well, I . . ."

His arms came from beneath her; he stretched her out on the plaid.

"Ouch!" yelped Mara.

"What's the matter?"

"There's something hard underneath me. A piece of rock, I think."

"Shove over a bit," said Roy, "and I'll get rid of it. Now lie back," he said, after doing so, "because there happens to be something hard above you as well."

It took a moment for his meaning to sink in.

"Roy!" she shrieked. "That's horribly vulgar."

"It was, wasn't it?" he returned complacently. "Something tells me—thanks to you—I'm going to turn into a very vulgar fellow. Do you mind?"

Mara giggled softly and pulled his face down to hers. "Not so long as I'm the one you're vulgar with," she admitted shamelessly.

"In that case, let us now be vulgar together," Roy invited, kissing her very hard.

Mara wriggled to get more underneath him and let out another shriek. "Ow! I thought you got rid of that piece of rock."

"I thought I did too. Look, move over here. I tell you what. *I'll* lie on the plaid this time and *you* lie on top of me."

Mara did as he suggested even while she asked in a small, doubtful voice, "Can we do it that way?"

"We'll soon find out," he answered at his most cheerful. "I don't see why not. A chap I knew at school had some pictures—well, never mind that . . ."

"What kind of pictures?" Mara asked suspiciously.

"Educational ones," Roy told her firmly. "Now stop talking, please. There's a time for talking and a time for—other things."

But he was the one who talked during the "other things," calling out her name again and again, calling her sweet and dear and wonderful, calling her his lady Mara.

Then, having proved to their mutual satisfaction that they *could* do it "that way," a bludgeoning could not have sent them into a deeper sleep.

They did not awaken until the morning sun came streaming through the front of their arbor, streaking across the faces of the two bodies entwined on the plaid.

It woke Roy first, and he lay still for a moment, trying to make sense of his surroundings. His memory came flooding back as soon as he looked down at the head against his shoulder and the mane of blue-black hair fanned out across his chest.

All of the memories.

One of his arms tightened possessively about her. With a single finger he stroked one velvet cheek, then the silken lashes of her closed eyes.

He could not feel the remorse that he knew he should feel. It should never have happened, but Lord, how fervently thankful he was that it had!

Still, she was not quite fifteen, just a child going to school in six months to be made a lady. It could not happen again, not for God knows how long. It was up to him to protect her. And since that meant he must protect her most of all from himself, he lay savoring the sweetness of the moment, knowing there would not, must not—perhaps for many years—be another like it.

"R-Roy?" she murmured sleepily.

He would say it one last time. "Yes, my lady Mara?"

She sat up suddenly, and he watched in tender amusement as she brushed herself off and combed out her hair with her fingers, nervously picked up the pit from her third peach and slipped it into her pocket, then neatly folded the paper wrappings from the sandwiches. She busied herself with a half-dozen needless chores, and all the while the blue-black mane swished back and forth, donkey-like, slap-slap against her shoulders.

It was he who leaned forward to take hold of her and make her look up into his eyes.

"Don't ever be ashamed, Mara. Don't ever be sorry. My brave beautiful girl, I am every bit as grateful to you this morning as I was last night." He pressed his lips to her hands. "As I will be the rest of my life."

When he saw her smile come out, like the sun bursting through the overhanging branches of their arbor, he knew he had guessed right about what troubled her.

"We had better go, Mara," he told her in

the same caressing voice. "I want to get you home before anyone becomes aware that you've been missing."

"Oh glory, yes!"

She sprang up and Roy jumped up too. They shook out the plaid together, then folded it, their hands touching as they brought the ends together. Her body swayed toward him, but Roy stepped back.

"No, Mara. And stop trying to tempt me, you witch!"

"Why not?"

"Someday, when you're all grown up, if you still want me to, I'll court you in style, but no more lovemaking till then."

"Why?"

"Because it would be wrong."

"Then why was last night right?" Mara asked him, her mouth quivering.

"Last night was special. Last night was different. Last night we were stuck high on a mountain, and I was crazily unhappy and blurted out to you why, and you were wildly, wonderfully generous to heal my hurts and cure what sickened me. You made me happier last night than I have ever been before, but now we've got to be sensible."

"Why?"

"For a reason that you, not I, pointed out to me when you were too young for urges. Men plant the seeds, you said, but girls get the babies."

Both Mara's hands flew to cover her

mouth. When she took them away again, "Oh, my goodness me!" she said in shock. "I completely forgot."

"We both did," said Roy a bit grimly, "but we mustn't ever again."

"Will I . . . do you suppose . . . last night?"

"You'll be fine," Roy told her quickly. "You have nothing to worry about from last night, but now that you're . . . It's different after the first time; you have to take special care. Understand?"

She nodded solemnly, and he threw the folded plaid across his shoulder and held out his hand. She gave him her own and they went down the mountain together, hand in hand even on the narrowest, trickiest part of the path.

Chapter Sixteen

ON MONDAY MORNING, A WEEK LATER, ROY came galloping up the side road to Treeways. Mara watched from the kitchen window as he stopped a moment to talk to Donnie and gave the reins of his mare over to him. She waited expectantly and with the new shyness she often felt now for him to come into the house.

She had seen him twice since their day on the mountain but never alone. Roy had helped Angus on the farm with all their workers about . . . Donnie had been with them when they rode . . . the whole family had been together at mealtime.

She had never before played what she called silly girls' games, but now she pretended not to be aware when he came into the kitchen. Almost as though he understood, he said "Hullo, Mara" as he kissed Mam's cheek, and when she looked up and

answered "Oh, hello" with seeming careless-
ness, he smiled a new rather sweet, grave
smile at her.

"I'm leaving for London tomorrow," he
said abruptly, and the cup that Mara was
carefully drying for the third time smashed
into bits on the kitchen floor.

"That's an even dozen this year," sighed
Emma as Mara stooped to pick up the pieces.

Roy squatted beside her. "Let me do that.
You'll cut yourself." He saw the trail of red
across her thumb. "You've *already* cut yourself. Damnation, Mara, you—"

Then he saw her face and the tears threat-
ening to spill out of her eyes. "I'll tend to
this," he said more gently. "Go stick your
finger in cold water and let Mam bind it up."

By the time the blood stopped flowing and
the thumb had been bandaged and the floor
cleaned of the smashed bits of the cup, Mara
was able to listen with apparent composure
to Roy's explanation.

"An express came from my father on Sat-
urday, instructing me to leave this morning
for London. I'm to live at Irwine House with
him till next spring, studying languages."

"Languages?" puzzled Emma. "I thought
you studied all you needed to know of them at
Eton."

"So did I," laughed Roy, "but they were
mostly the dead ones. I also had instruction
in French, which I already knew from my
French governess, and I picked up a bit of

Spanish—private tutoring—thought it might be useful in the army. Well, it seems the Baf—Dr. Keate told my father, in his expulsion letter, no less, that I had a real gift for languages. His Grace mentioned it to someone at the War Office he was speaking to about a commission for me. Well, that someone told someone else who told someone else . . . and the long and short of it is that I'm assured of a really good position if my French meets their requirements and I can improve my Spanish. My father has a tutor waiting for me in London. The only reason I didn't leave this morning, as he directed, is that I wanted to say good-bye to you all *and* have one last day out with Mara. Is that all right, Mam?"

"Well, I suppose you'll hardly be any good to me with that cut finger, Mara," said Emma, "so best go change your clothes. Will you eat supper with us, laddie?" she asked Roy.

"Miss my farewell supper? Not likely. Wear the new blue habit with the hat," he called after Mara.

When she came back, dressed in the new blue habit, Emma and Roy were on the veranda; Donnie had brought the horses round. They were still discussing the supper menu.

"Roast beef and Yorkshire pudding, too, I suppose," said Emma, pretending to be put out.

"Of course. And don't forget the pie,

please," he shouted back as he and Mara mounted their horses.

As they cantered along together, Mara sat very straight and silent until they were out of sight of Treeways. Then he put out one hand to take her reins and bring Arrow and his mare to a complete halt.

She glared at him angrily. "I thought you wanted to ride."

"I do—as soon as you calm down."

"I'm perfectly calm."

"The hell you are!" Roy exploded. "Come on, Mara. What are you simmering about? That I'm going to London? Do you think I'm betraying you by going?"

Since that was precisely what she did think but couldn't bring herself to admit, Mara continued to sit in stiff and injured silence.

Roy walked his mare in front of Arrow, so she couldn't avoid facing him.

"Look at me," he said harshly. "I said look at me, Mara. What else do you expect me to do? You know the army's going to be my career, and this is the first step. Do you want me to turn it down and play around in Cumberland till it's time for you to go to school? *You'd* be leaving *me* then. You're not even fifteen; I'm barely eighteen. For most of the next few years we'll have no choice but to keep leaving each other. You don't think you can come with me, do you, or that they'd let us set up house together?"

Mara turned her head a little, the first encouraging sign that she was listening.

"Mara," he said urgently, "one can't turn the clock back; there's no way of returning to yesterday. After what happened on the mountain, I can't stay near you all the time, not even a *little* of the time without—without—for God's sakes, I want it to happen again!" he cried out in such genuine anguish that the last trace of pain from his supposed abandonment vanished from around her heart.

"It mustn't happen again," he said more quietly. "It can't. You know why as well as I."

"Yes, Roy," Mara said, her voice very subdued but not the least bit sad now. The eyes that met his were shiningly bright. "I'm sorry," she told him. "I was acting silly."

"You were," he told her frankly. "Very silly."

"It's just," she began apologetically, "that I thought—"

"I know exactly what you thought, and you were *damn* silly." He put out his hand to cover both of hers. "I'm coming back, Mara. No matter how many years it takes, I'm coming back."

They rode along the river Eden, laughing loud and long in their relief. They sang bawdy songs beloved of Etonians—Mara knew them all. They talked about Duggie and school, Emma and Angus and Donnie,

Treeways and Rydale and Dumfries, Sir Cuthbert and Griselda; about the duke, his father, her Grace, his mother, his three handsome brothers; about everything except making love on a mountain while lying on top of his plaid. A plaid now folded away in her cupboard with other treasures. And neither did they talk about parting or separation or good-bye.

When they left the river path, Roy slightly in the lead, Mara noticed that he had branched off from their usual road. "Did you mean to go a different way?" she asked him, catching up.

"Yes." Evidently deciding this answer was inadequate, after a few seconds he added, "We're not picnicking today. I'm taking you to lunch at an inn."

"Oh, lovely. Where?"

Roy swallowed, staring straight ahead.

"Gretna Green."

"Gretna *Green!*"

"You've heard of it?"

"Of course. It's where all the runaways go to be married. As a matter of fact, Mam and Da—well, they weren't runaways, of course, but it *was* an elopement—they were married at Gretna over the anvil. How jolly! Maybe we'll be lucky and get to see the ceremony for an elopement. I always wanted to be at a blacksmith's when he performed a marriage."

"You're in luck then," said Roy a bit grimly. "I know of a marriage that's been arranged for a runaway couple in less than an hour from now."

"If it's an elopement, how can you know?"

"Because," said Roy quite calmly now, "*I* arranged it and the eloping couple is us."

Mara reined in her horse, and so did he. She stared at him, gulped a little, then said very positively, "You're Bedlam-mad."

"We *have* to get married, Mara," Roy told her.

"*Have* to?"

"Yes, I lied to you the other morning because I didn't want you to be frightened. The truth is that you could have started a baby already. It doesn't only happen *after* the first time. It's possible anytime a man and woman are together. That means any one of our three times . . ."

His voice faded away under her dumbfounded stare. Then he repeated with conviction, "We *have* to get married. I'm not going to risk your reputation."

Mara dug her teeth so hard into her underlip that a drop of blood appeared. "We could —we could—" She bent her head, but he could see one very pink cheek and the scarlet tip of an ear. "In about ten days I'll know for sure. We could wait until then . . . to see if it's needful, I mean. If it was, *then* I could write to tell you. . . ."

"And what excuse could I give for returning to Dumfries just two weeks after I got to

London? If I told the truth, you can be sure I wouldn't be allowed to come. If I didn't, I probably *would* have to run away.

"Besides—" He scowled fiercely, not at her but at the need to explain. "Ah, hell, Mara," he groaned out, "you're not an ordinary miss-ish schoolgirl. I have to put it plainly. If you *have* started a baby, the earlier the date on our wedding lines, the better for you. If we delayed till I went to London and came back, it would be well over a month between . . . well, between the bedding and the wedding. I'm damned if I want all the ladies in fashionable London counting on their fingers after a child is born."

"But what if we marry and there isn't a baby?"

"Simple. *Then* I'll go to my father, and he'll arrange a quiet annulment. No one will ever need to know."

"What's an annulment?"

"To annul is to cancel out. So an annulment is a way the law provides to wipe out a marriage and say it never really existed."

He leaned forward and grabbed her hair, giving it a tug that pulled Mara toward him. He kissed the tip of her nose. "The annulment will protect *me* from being permanently trapped into marriage with a designing hussy like you," he said lightly. "And the marriage will protect *you* from loss of reputation at the hands of an unprincipled rake like me."

Mara gave an uncharacteristic nervous giggle. "It all sounds rather complicated going through a marriage."

"The results if we don't could be even more complicated."

"Well, I suppose . . ."

"You suppose right. Let's get to it."

As soon as she gave a brief, doubtful nod, they rode on.

"There's just one thing I have to tell you, Mara, that may be a disappointment," Roy mentioned a few minutes after they crossed the border into Scotland.

She looked over at him anxiously.

"I had no idea you cherished this burning desire to see a marriage performed by a blacksmith or I certainly would have made my arrangements with one. As it is, we're to be married by a toll keeper about a mile down this road. Do you mind? I picked Mr. Renfrew for the very practical reason that the inn where I ordered lunch is quite near the toll house. Also, he's rather elderly—both his hearing and his eyesight seemed deficient—so I hoped he wouldn't notice that you are slightly younger than I claimed. Speaking of which—" He halted his horse and signaled for her to do the same. "Bundle your hair on top of your head and put on your bonnet. It will make you look older. That's why I wanted you to wear your new habit and hat; they add at least six months to your age."

Mara giggled again, but this time not nervously as she yanked off her ribbon, twisted her hair in a big knot, and used the ribbon as a band to keep her hair up. Then she put on her bonnet, tying it demurely under her chin with a big bow.

She crossed her arms over her breast, bent her head a little, then peeped flirtatiously up at him. "Do I look like a bride?" she asked in a sugary-sweet little-girl voice.

"Baggage." He thumped her affectionately on one shoulder. "Come. On to Gretna."

Chapter Seventeen

WHEN THEY REACHED THE TOLL HOUSE AND Roy came around to help her down from Arrow, he put his hands on her waist and swung her to the ground, whispering in her ear, "You may not look like any bride, but you look like *my* bride."

Before the startled Mara could frame an answer, he was hustling her forward to be introduced to two resplendently dressed exquisites a little older than himself, both almost identically garbed in shining black Hessians, buff breeches, dark green riding coats, and tall hats.

"My friends, Lord Sterling, Marquis of Blane, and Mr. Frederick Corley, who will serve as our witnesses. Gentlemen, my promised bride, Miss Mara Rydale."

"How could you be so silly?" demanded Mara in a fierce whisper as they all hurried forward into the toll house. "What

kind of secret will it be if all your friends
know?"

"Not all," Roy answered imperturbably.
"Just these two, who were staying near
enough—Yorkshire—to be summoned here
in time."

"I still say—"

"Well, don't say it," he interrupted amiably. "They gave me their word never to speak
of it, except for your or my need. Do hush,
Mara," he said, as she seemed ready to continue the argument. "In the event of that
need," he added significantly, "I wanted witnesses who were above reproach—not casual
passersby."

"Oh!" said Mara.

"Exactly, oh!" mimicked Roy, linking her
arm through his.

The toll keeper, Mr. Renfrew, a grizzled
gnome of a man, was as old and debilitated
as Roy had described him. His wife was
much younger, much bigger, much rounder
and rosier.

"Come, Dad," she addressed her husband
in tones of brisk fondness. "Here's the young
couple come to be wed."

Mara and Roy stood facing him with young
Lord Sterling and Mr. Corley standing behind them.

"Now you're here to be wed and I'm here to
do the marrying," quavered Mr. Renfrew,
"so the only question is, are you both willing?
Are you willing, lassie?"

For the first time in her life Mara's ever-ready tongue clove to the roof of her mouth. "She's willing," Roy said after twenty seconds of dead silence.

"She got to say so for herself to make it all shipshape," Mr. Renfrew reproved him peevishly.

Roy pinched the elbow of his paralyzed bride-to-be. "For God's sakes, say you're willing!"

Mara's voice was as quavery as the toll keeper's. "I'm w-w-willing."

"And you, young feller, what did you say your name was?"

"Lord Raleigh Irwine."

"Lord Raleigh Irwine. You hear that, Aileen? A real live lord. Well, Lord Raleigh Irwine, am I correct that you're in favor of marrying yon lassie? If you are, put the ring on her finger."

"I, Lord Raleigh Irwine," said Roy rapidly, catching hold of Mara's icy hand and slipping a gold band onto her third finger, "take you, Mara Rydale, to be my wedded wife, to love and to honor and cherish so long as we both shall live."

Outside a coach horn blew, and the toll keeper deserted bride and bridegroom to thrust his head through a small window.

"Hold yer lugs!" he shouted. "I'm performing a wedding."

He returned to the bridal pair and addressed Roy scoldingly, "You didn't have to be saying all that, me lord. I'm the one gets to say that by Scots law you're now wedded nice and tight for the rest of your natural lives, the same as if you had it done in church."

After he came back from collecting the coach toll, Mr. Renfrew entered the marriage into his record book, but Roy had him sign two pages from a roll of paper he took from an inside pocket of his jacket. Two other copies were signed by Lord Sterling and Mr. Corley.

Mr. Renfrew's faded blue eyes having been made to gleam with pleasure at the feel of the coins Roy pressed into his gnarled palm, the new-wedded lord returned to his bride's side.

"Now you really are my lady Mara," he said softly, lifting the hand that bore his wedding ring.

"Gracious goodness, is *that* what I'm supposed to be called?"

"Well, no." He reddened a little. "Actually, the proper name is Lady Raleigh," he mumbled.

"Lady *Raleigh*," repeated his wife of five minutes, her eyes brimful of Mara mischief.

"But Lady Roy would be acceptable." Her husband's minatory look proclaimed that Lady Roy would not only be acceptable but mandatory.

"Lady *Roy*," mused Mara. "Lady *Raleigh* . . . I don't know which I prefer."

"I *do,*" said Roy emphatically, swatting her on the backside to the horror of his friends.

Mara, who was quite accustomed to being on the giving as well as the receiving end of such swats with Duggie and Donnie as well as with Roy, looked around as Mr. Corley's eyes bulged and Lord Sterling exclaimed protestingly, "My dear fellow!"

"I don't know what possessed me to marry the brute!" she told them soulfully.

"Or I you, minx!"

Seeing the exchange of grins between the bridal pair, Roy's friends grinned in turn, deciding this was all good sport.

Most girls, in their opinion, were *not* good sport. When they were young, they were hidden away in the nursery. Once they came out, they had to be treated as though they were made of easily broken porcelain and spoken to as though they were fragile flowers, who might fade away or fall apart at a rough gesture or a strong word.

They looked wistfully at Mara when the four of them got to the fence where all their horses had been tied. She unknotted her reins, climbed the fence, and mounted Arrow unaided, without—they noticed—so much as a look at Roy to indicate that she needed, wanted, or expected help.

"Come on." Roy led the way past the toll house. "I ordered a marvelous wedding lunch for us, and we're a little past the time I gave. The innkeeper will be wondering where we are."

"What you mean is"—Mara galloped on ahead, and her teasing voice came floating back to the other three—"you don't want all the good food you're thinking of so greedily to spoil."

"Damn right!" Roy called out. "Mara, don't race, it's only a few yards more down the road."

She reined in till they caught up with her, and they all proceeded together at a gentle trot until they arrived at the inn.

Their luncheon, which was laid out in a private parlor, had by no means spoiled. It was ready on a long trestle table in satisfying abundance. Two tureens of hot soup, onion and a Scotch broth. Baked fish, buttered crabs, broiled lobster. A saddle of mutton and a platter of cold meats. Potatoes roasted in their jackets, pickled onions and peas, and a variety of garden vegetables. Puddings and custards. Tea and ale. Oven-warm breads and scones and mounds of fresh-churned butter and preserves.

"I say!" said Mr. Corley.

"A feast for the gods." Surreptitiously, Lord Sterling undid the buttons of his waistcoat.

"Fill your plates and come to the table. I said we would prefer to serve ourselves."

"Jolly good idea," approved Mr. Corley.

"After you, Lady Ral—Roy!" amended Lord Sterling with an apologetic look at his friend as he handed her a soup bowl.

Mara filled the bowl from the tureen of onion soup and tore off a chunk of bread, then sat down at the round table in the center of the room all set for four. It was a happy, noisy meal. Taking their cue from Lady Roy's husband, his two friends treated her like one of them. They laughed and joked and talked, without inhibition, all of them jumping up periodically to refill their plates with enormous amounts of food, which they put away with the greatest of ease.

After enough ale to make them careless of a lady's presence, the three old Etonians began singing some of the bawdier songs they had learned at school. Only two of them were a bit shocked when Mara joined in the singing.

"Not very proper for a lady," said Mr. Corley, blinking at her owlishly.

"Very improper," chimed in Lord Sterling.

"But Roy taught them to me, and he's my husband," she pointed out virtuously.

"Husband's got a right," said Mr. Corley to Lord Sterling.

"I suppose so," said Lord Sterling dubiously. "M'mother used to do what my father said . . . when he was alive . . . she did."

"Anyhow, I'm not a lady," said Mara. "I'm only fi—ow!" She glared at Roy who, under the table, had kicked her not the least bit gently in the shin.

He glared right back, leaning toward her, pretending to straighten her jacket collar. "Keep your dear little tongue in your dear big mouth," he advised softly.

The innkeeper offered a happy diversion by entering their private parlor carrying a small three-tiered wedding cake iced in white. A serving maid just behind him bore a bottle of champagne in a bucket of ice.

The serving maid cleared the table while the innkeeper opened and poured the champagne. Mara removed the sprig of tiny flowers on top of the cake and carefully set it beside her plate.

"What's that, Mara?" asked Lord Sterling.

"White heather. Much rarer in Scotland than the purplish kind." She smiled forgivingly at Roy. "It's supposed to bring good fortune."

He smiled back at her, his new sweet serious smile. "My good fortune," said Roy, as though only the two of them were at the table, "came in the toll house two hours ago."

Mara's smile faded; her hand trembled as she cut the cake. She found herself wishing with an intensity that shocked her to the core that the two of them *were* alone—alone and on their mountain!

Roy's hand came down over hers; he

helped her cut the four generous slices of cake. As they cut, she felt the quivering of his palm, the throbbing pulse at his wrist, and her heart leaped with happiness. Then she *wasn't* wanton; she need not be ashamed. Whatever thoughts or feelings she had could not be wrong, not when it was obvious that he shared every one.

Just before they left their luncheon parlor, Roy took out his roll of papers and asked the little serving maid to bring pen and ink.

"I have two papers for you to sign, Mara," he told her.

She looked over his shoulder. "What do they say?"

"They're both the same, one copy for you and one for me. I had an attorney prepare them. It just says that on this day, Malcolm Renfrew, toll keeper in the village of Gretna Green, Scotland, joined Mara Rydale of Treeways Cottage and Rydale Park, England, and Lord Raleigh Irwine of Dumfries Castle, in marriage."

"What about the others?"

"Tom and Freddie signed an affidavit that they witnessed our marriage. Mr. Renfrew attests that he performed the marriage."

The maid came in with a quill and a bottle of ink and Mara waited till she was gone to inquire, "Why so many?"

"Evidence," said Roy tersely. "Testimony. One set for you, one for me. If my carriage

overturns on the road to London . . . if anything happens ever . . . I don't want any
doubt to exist *ever* that you and I were well
and truly married."

He turned toward his friends. "Understood?"

They nodded solemnly.

He turned back to Mara. Her lips were
pressed tightly together; she was visibly
trembling.

"I said 'if,'" he reminded her with exasper-
ated affection. "Nothing's going to happen to
me. I'm just taking precautions like a responsible married man. Right, chaps?"

His friends nodded solemnly again, and
Mara couldn't help laughing. "You sound
like three regular Benedicts," she flung at
them over her shoulder as she signed where
Roy indicated, right under his own signature.

While Roy settled the shot, his friends left
the private parlor, and each one returned in
minutes bearing a wrapped parcel.

"This was my grandmother's, dear Lady
Roy," said Lord Sterling, presenting his gift
with a graceful bow. "I hope it gives you as
much pleasure as it did her."

Frederick Corley, with a blush and a much
less graceful bow, presented his own offering. "Asked m'sister what a lady might
like . . . didn't mention any names, of
course," he assured her.

Lord Sterling's gift was an old hand-painted heart-shaped music box that played several English folk songs.

"Oh, it's lovely, lovely," Mara told him. "I shall treasure it always, even more because it was your grandmother's."

Mr. Corley's gift was a mother-of-pearl jewelry box.

"It's beautiful, Freddy," she told him earnestly, and the use of his given name caused him to blush harder than ever. "The first precious things I'll put into it are my marriage lines."

They parted after Roy had wrung their hands and thanked them, too, his friends deciding to spend the night at the inn and leave for home the next day.

Silently, casting shy looks at one another now and then, Mara and Roy galloped out of Gretna Green and crossed the border back to England.

At their first rest near a stream where they stopped to water the horses, Roy took a fine-linked gold chain from his waistcoat pocket.

"You won't be able to wear your wedding ring when you get home," he said. "I thought you might like to wear it around your neck— on this."

"Yes," said Mara, accepting the chain. "I would like that, thank you." She bit at her lip. "I'm sorry I have nothing for you."

"Mara, I thought we already settled that.

You gave me my gift, remember? High on a mountain?"

Mara blushed furiously and cast about for a change of subject. "How shall I—what shall I—if I have something to tell you, what shall I do?"

"I'll write to you from Irwine House the moment I get to London. Write back, and if there's going to be a child, include a sentence that says . . . oh, something like 'It's fortunate we crossed the border on our last ride.' I'll understand."

"And if I'm all right. If there isn't a baby coming?"

"Then say something that's just the opposite . . . like, 'Our lunch at the inn was jolly, but we didn't really have to go all the way to Scotland.' I'll understand that, too."

"And you'll speak to your father about an annulment?"

"Yes."

"And you'll let me know right away if we're not married anymore?"

"If we're not married anymore," Roy told her teasingly, "after me, you'll be the first to know."

Chapter Eighteen

OWING TO THE VAGARIES OF NATURE, IT WAS A full month—more than double the expected time—before Mara was able to send the promised message off to London.

I was thinking of what a lovely time we had the day you introduced me to your friends, she wrote, *but as it turns out, we might just as well have had our lunch at an inn our side of the border.*

Roy had all but given up hope of any such news and was braced for the inevitable confrontation with his father. He ought to be relieved, he knew, reading over the careful *P. S. Will you speak to the duke?"* He *must* be relieved, he admonished himself. To father a child at nineteen; to be saddled with the responsibilities of a husband and parent right at the start of his career! It would have been calamitous.

Under the impetus of these self-reminders,

he seized a sheet of paper and wrote swiftly. *Your letter was most reassuring. Regarding the matter you mentioned, I addressed my father and he has his attorneys looking into it. There might be some delay, however, as the mills of the law grind exceeding slowly.*

The mills of the law were so very dilatory that, as it happened, Mara was attending Miss Petersham's Seminary for Young Ladies in Bath before she received a cautious aside in the middle of his chatty monthly letter.

The cancellation of the ceremony that concerned you has been attended to finally, and all is well now.

"I'm glad. Of course, I'm glad. I *must* be," Mara told herself, unknowingly echoing Roy.

She would not let herself wonder why—if she were so glad—there was a dull ache, a terrible weight of heaviness about her heart as she unhooked the gold chain from around her neck. Suspended from it, always tucked out of sight inside her chemise, were a plain narrow wedding band and a small ornamental key.

She had no right to wear the ring now—not even around her neck.

With the ornamental key, she unlocked the mother-of-pearl jewelry box that Frederick Corley had presented to her at her wedding lunch a half-year before. It contained only the papers Lord Raleigh Irwine had given her as evidence that a wedding had taken place between them. Her marriage lines and affidavits . . . some white heather . . . and a dried peach pit.

It was the custom in ancient times for a lord or knight to give his lady a first-day gift in return for the great gift she had given him in the night.

How vividly she could see him . . . on one knee . . . holding out the peach. *My lady Mara, this is my gift to you.*

"It's over," said Mara aloud. "Time to get on with my life. If he has no regrets, then neither shall I."

It helped that Griselda had been right about Miss Petersham's school. Mara found herself happy there. Since the pupils included the daughters of the middle class, not just fashionable young ladies, the studies and students alike were more interesting to her than would have been the case in the generality of such seminaries.

A tutor was available to further her classical studies, and her interest in these subjects was not considered odd, any more than it was odd for Margaret Ponsonby to spend most of her time poring over history books so that when she left school she might act as secretary to her father, who was a famous historian. Or for Diane De Montford, whose mother had danced before the Czar of all the Russias, to have the use of an empty attic room, where she practiced ballet exercises at a bar before a specially set-up room-length mirror.

At the end of June, Mara returned from Bath to spend what her father had made very clear would be her last free summer at Treeways. From now on, when she returned home from school holidays, home was Rydale Park.

It was by no means the carefree, happy summer Mara had visualized. There was no possibility that Roy would be coming to Dumfries. His last letter to Bath had breezily informed her that he was on his way to the Peninsula as an aide to none other than Viscount Wellington, in Spain at the head of the British Expeditionary Forces.

Duggie *did* come home from Eton, but only for a month. Sir Cuthbert's attorney, acting on his client's behalf, had fulfilled the promise made to Emma before his bastard son's birth. He had been educated like a gentleman; a lieutenant's commission had now been purchased for him in a hussar regiment. The remainder of his future was in his own hands.

Duggie would be leaving for the Peninsula, too, soon.

Even while they milked cows, curried horses, frolicked and rode together, Mara would sometimes have moments of panicked breathlessness. It seemed to her that not only the life she loved but the people she most cherished were all slipping away from her one by one.

The day that Duggie left, she and Emma

and Nurse cried quietly together in the kitchen. Later, after a silent, solemn lunch—even Angus and Donnie could not pretend to much gaiety—Mara rode out alone. By the banks of the river Eden, she sat, weeping wildly, mourning for the brother who had just left, the lover who had gone before, and the untrammeled joys of childhood that she knew instinctively would never be hers again.

The next two years at Miss Petersham's passed busily and more happily than Mara would have believed. In spite of living at Rydale, when she went back to Cumbria, she was so often at Treeways that she hardly felt the loss of her dear foster family.

Letters came from Duggie almost every month, but she no longer heard from Roy more than three or four times a year. Sometimes she felt that what had been between them had happened only in a dream . . . or perhaps never happened at all.

She would lock the door of the bedroom that was still hers at Treeways, and from the bottom of the cupboard she would take out the wool plaid on which Roy and she had picnicked . . . on which he and she had . . .

She would spread the plaid on her bed and put the music box that had once belonged to Lord Sterling's grandmother on top of it. She would open it, listening to the tinkling of the music while she unlocked the mother-of-pearl jewelry box and gently sorted out the contents . . . a wedding band on a gold chain, the papers to prove she had once been briefly married, some crumbling white heather, and the dearest thing of all to her, a dried peach pit that brought back the sweetest memories of all.

There was a grand neighborhood party at Rydale to celebrate her eighteenth birthday. The day after it Mara rode to Treeways for a private celebration with her family who, of course, had not been invited to the grander event with the gentry. Instead, they had celebrated Donnie's birthday without her.

There were gifts for her from all the Mac-Tavishes and Nurse, including a white lace mantilla that Duggie had sent from Spain with an affectionate note.

"And this"—Emma produced another wrapped parcel as they lingered at table eating the cake especially made for this second-in-a-row birthday supper—"is from Roy. It was in the box he sent me a few months ago; he asked me to save it for you."

Mara unwrapped the soft bundle handed over to her. It contained a Spanish shawl—a huge square of heavy silk with blue roses on a black background and a thick black fringe all around.

"Oh, my, it's magnificent!" said Emma.

"Try it on, my dearie," urged Nurse.

Mara stood up and threw the shawl about her shoulders.

"Like a queen you look," pronounced Angus, waxing unusually poetic.

"I doubt the Queen has one so fine," Nurse said loyally.

Donnie, bored by this fashion talk, lifted his eyes heavenward and reached for a second piece of cake. Mara smiled and asked him a question about Betty, his new prize cow. Immediately he had plenty to say, and the subject of the shawl from Roy was not mentioned again until Emma and Mara were alone in the kitchen washing up.

"Roy wrote that the mixture of blue and black in the shawl reminded him of your hair."

"He said it to you, I notice," Mara answered in a tight, hard voice. "He had nothing to say to me. Six months since his last letter and not so much as a message to go with the gift."

"Mara, he's far away . . . and a soldier. It's a strange life they lead, all those men in distant lands, away from their own, often facing dangers we can't understand. They forget . . . I think . . . the little things important to us at home. I don't find it strange Roy neglected a message with the shawl; I think the wonder is he remembered your birthday at all."

"I must remember to tell him so when I write my thanks," said Mara lightly, overbrightly, unconvinced.

The next morning at breakfast Griselda said hesitantly to her stepdaughter, "Mara, your father and I have talked it over. If you would like to be presented in London, we are both willing to give you a season in town."

Mara looked at them in great surprise. She knew that her father did not care at all for London and Griselda disliked the fashionable life, if not the town. She was always happiest with her husband at Rydale.

Strangely touched by the sacrifice they were offering and grateful that she felt no temptation to accept it, Mara shook her head.

"Gracious goodness," she said merrily, "the only ones who would hate a London presentation more than *me* would be the two of you."

"You're sure?" Sir Cuthbert asked her gruffly. "It's true I think the whole business is a lot of nonsense . . . plenty of husbands to be found without girls hieing off to London in search of society fops in starched shirtpoints and striped waistcoats. Still, Griselda says you should have your chance if you want it. My only daughter. My only . . . it's right you should be presented, if you wish."

"But I *don't* wish," Mara persisted gently. "I thank you both"—she smiled across at Griselda—"but I truly don't care about a London debut. I agree with you, Sir Cuthbert." She turned back to her father. "I don't want a London fop in starched shirtpoints and a striped waistcoat. I'm sure the counties hereabouts will provide plenty of husband material when I'm ready for one, which at present I'm not. To be truthful, if you are willing, I would be pleased to spend another half-year at Miss Petersham's."

This proposal was so pleasing to both her father and Griselda that shortly she was on her way back to Bath, though the new course of study she was planning would have shocked both of them to the core.

The doctor who attended the young ladies at Miss Petersham's had indicated last year —on being strongly solicited—that he would be glad to teach her the rudiments of treatment for cases of emergency, cuts and bruises, dislocations and other injuries, even, perhaps, midwifery.

"Such things as a soldier's wife might find it useful to know," Mara had explained to him earnestly.

The good doctor had tactfully never asked why Miss Mara Rydale of Rydale Park felt the need to learn so many things that could only prove to be an asset in the education of an ordinary soldier's wife.

Chapter Nineteen

IN MAY 1814, SIX WEEKS BEFORE MARA WAS
scheduled to leave Miss Petersham's permanently and return home to Cumberland, her
father's old traveling coach arrived in Bath
and stopped, as directed by Sir Cuthbert's
attorney, at the Ship Inn. The old coachman,
Gardner, and a powerfully built young groom
descended from the box and Griselda's maid,
Maggie, from inside the coach.

Rather wistfully leaving the other two to a
bit of hot supper, Gardner set off at once for
the seminary to see the young lady.

When Mara came into the parlor where
guests were received, a little pale and
breathless from hurrying, she asked at once,
"Something is wrong, Gardner?"

Silently, he held out the black-bordered
envelope, and she tore it open with shaking
fingers.

My dear Miss Mara,

It is with deep regret I inform you that your stepmother died yesterday of injuries suffered in a fall on the hunting field.

Your father is overcome with grief and unable to write but desired me to hurry your homecoming.

Indeed, he needs you sorely, the more so that he is not a man to show his feelings, despite being in a state of great affliction.

You may safely leave the details of the journey in Gardner's hands. All inn arrangements have been made, and he has the necessary monies.

Your hmble. obdt. Servant,
James Firkin, Atty.-at-law

It was a nightmare journey. They started out each day shortly after dawn and traveled as long as daylight permitted. The traveling coach was built for endurance but was not well sprung, and Mara was tossed and shaken about till she felt bruised and bone-weary enough to weep. Maggie, beside her, sobbed ceaselessly for the dear-loved mistress she had maided these twenty years.

A more welcome sight than the gates of Rydale Mara could not remember, though her heart sank when she recollected that she must now face and offer consolation to her father.

How history repeated itself! Only a dozen years ago she had been sent for when her own mother died. But *that,* she recalled sadly, had not required much fortitude on anyone's part. How sad that a mother, wife, and daughter should have been so little mourned. How sad that Mara Rydale grieved for her stepmother more than she had for Lady Mary. But Lady Mary had been almost a stranger. She had come to know and love Griselda well.

It was immediately plain to Mara that, even while they drank endless cups of his tea and ate the funeral cakes he provided, most of his neighbors could not like Sir Cuthbert, though they might agree among themselves that his life had been singularly marked out by misfortune. A wife who could give him only a still-born son, then a daughter . . . a second wife who was barren. Even his wives —so much younger than he, both of them— had not managed to survive him.

If he had proclaimed his grief loudly, they might have warmed to sympathy, but he was such a cold, contained stick of a man. He neither showed nor felt, they decided uncharitably, any grief and he would probably look about him as quickly for wife number three as he had for wife number two.

They were woefully mistaken. Sir Cuthbert would not for any consideration take another wife. He was nearing his fifty-second birthday. By the time his year's mourning— genuine mourning this time—was done with, he would be three and fifty. Not too late, physically, to beget a son, but the chance of being present to raise him to manhood was far slimmer.

He had no inclination to go through that business again—the courting, the wedding, the month-to-month expectation, the hopes dashed, and even should there be a full-term pregnancy, always the possibility of another daughter.

In truth, he didn't desire another wife. He would never find one to suit him so well as his Griselda, his dear, homely, wonderful Griselda, the unexpected gift of his middle years.

When he wanted a woman, a serving wench or housemaid would serve his needs, or he would set up another mistress the likes of Millie Sloan, long ago pensioned off to live near her children in Scotland.

Mara would get the estate and monies; the baronetcy would die. The Rydale name, he decided in a burst of inspiration, need not die with it any more than the Rydale blood.

The obsession to get himself a son, which had colored the years of Sir Cuthbert's marriage to Lady Mary, had been submerged in loving understanding when Griselda proved to be barren. Now, heightened by a sense of sorrow and loss almost too great to be borne, the obsession had reemerged in a slightly different form. He would have his sons by proxy, by God! His daughter would provide them.

Mara was a fine, healthy, sensible girl, utterly unlike her mother. She would give him grandsons, and it would be for him to see that the grandsons bore the Rydale name.

They would be all-Rydale blood, his grandsons; he would marry his daughter to a Rydale descendant in the female line willing to take back the name.

He wove his plans as an antidote for grief and, without revealing them, as soon as the last mourner left his house, he empowered Mr. Firkin to track down every female Rydale connection, most of them hitherto ignored. He was particularly to discover, Sir Cuthbert ordered, which of them had sons.

The attorney was left with the impression that his client might be planning to adopt a likely descendant willing to adopt the Rydale name. It made him more glad than ever of the private meeting he had recently held with Miss Mara.

"By marriage settlement, Lady Rydale's jointure was hers alone, not only to use as she saw fit during her lifetime but to dispose of as she wished at her death. An earlier will in the first year of her marriage divided it among her nieces and nephews. A later will gave half to you."

"Griselda left me her money!"

"Half her money," Mr. Firkin corrected. "Eight thousand pounds in the funds. Also the house in London your father purchased for her shortly after they were married."

"Why would he do that? They neither of them liked living in London."

"Your father was sixteen years older than Lady Rydale; he never expected to survive her. He thought that when Rydale came to *you*, she should have a home of her own near her family connections. All these years it has been rented out for income, as it can continue to be."

"How dear of Griselda. When," asked Mara practically, "is the money mine? Right now?"

"Not until the youngest nephew reaches his majority, some five years from now. The house, though, is yours when you are one and twenty."

Mara smiled cheerily. "Well, it's a comfortable thought in the back of my mind for the future, but no use thinking about it now. And Sir Cuthbert has always been generous with money," she added with unconscious emphasis.

The third week in June, little more than a month after Griselda's funeral, Sir Cuthbert left Rydale. "A matter of business," he told Mara gruffly, announcing his journey. "If you want to spend the time at Treeways, I have no objection. I'll send for you on my return."

"Thank you, Father." She had taken to calling him that since Griselda's death. "I would prefer Treeways to staying alone here," she added calmly, not wishing to pain him—if she *could* pain him—by too great a show of delight.

The gloom of Rydale since her stepmother's death had been as oppressive as the mourning clothes husband, stepdaughter, and servants wore. Though she grieved for Griselda sincerely, she yearned to be away from crepe hangings, black garments, and, even more, the dark pall of depression that hung over the house.

"I suppose I should get you some sort of—no, you're too old for a governess . . . some sort of chaperone." Sir Cuthbert seemed to be speaking more to himself than to her.

"Gracious goodness, no!" Mara spoke up decidedly. "Only the poor lady you hired could dislike that more than me."

Sir Cuthbert smiled faintly for the first time since he had lost his wife.

Encouraged by the smile, Mara added firmly, "I shall go on very well as I am. When you are home, what need have I for a chaperone? And when I am at Treeways, I assure you that Emma is far stricter with me than Griselda ever was."

She had mentioned Griselda deliberately, feeling that it was no tribute to a loved one to wipe her name and memory out of conversation. She saw with satisfaction that Sir Cuthbert's face had softened considerably.

Nevertheless, two days later, the moment her father's carriage turned the corner of the driveway, she went directly to the stables for Arrow and was off to Treeways, her heart considerably lightened.

Sir Cuthbert's summons home came two weeks later, and Mara put off her gay flowered muslin, donned her mourning again, and returned to Rydale in the carriage that had been sent for her, a groom following with her horse.

Her father seemed much more cheerful, though he kept himself occupied with affairs of the estate and seemed to have to go to Carlisle more frequently than usual to see his attorney, Mr. Firkin.

Mara gradually established her own routine. Immediately after breakfast she met with Mrs. Bostwick, the housekeeper Griselda had brought with her to Rydale.

Acting on Emma's advice, "I am in your hands, Mrs. Bostwick," she had confessed frankly to that stately lady. "I know nothing about the management of an establishment like this. I cannot take the place of Lady Rydale, of course," she continued tactfully, "but I would be grateful if you would teach me how to go on."

Pleased by this approach, Mrs. Bostwick graciously consented to begin Mara's education as the present and future mistress of Rydale.

The remainder of each morning was spent in her private sitting room, occupied with the education she preferred, her reading in French, her study of Spanish.

She practiced her medical skills on any housemaid who fell ill or any tenant's child or stable boy who suffered a fall. To her regret, no baby was born on the estate, so there was no chance to use her midwifery.

In the afternoons she rode and walked, and at least twice a week she went to Treeways.

In the evenings, after an unfashionably early country dinner, Sir Cuthbert and his daughter had formed the habit of going into the library, which both preferred to the drawing room. Her father would drink his wine and do his accounts, and Mara would curl up in the big armchair with one of the delightful novels from Griselda's collection, helping herself as she read to countless cups of tea and innumerable small cakes and tarts from the tea tray.

In July her father departed on another short journey and Mara again went home to Treeways. She was there late in the month when word came from abroad that Wellington's Peninsular Army was being disbanded.

The cottage was wildly elated at the prospect that Duggie might come home for a long visit. Possibly Roy, too.

Mara could think and speak of Duggie's probable return with wholehearted joy. When she thought of Roy—Lord Raleigh Irwine, who incredibly, once and briefly, had been her husband—her thoughts were such a jumble of dread and anticipation, anger and expectation, resentment and longing, she almost wished that he would not come.

Almost.

Very early the next morning she left a note in the kitchen that she would be gone for the day and rode Arrow to Ambleside, galloping along the river road, then past the shepherd's hut where she and he had stopped for directions, the field where they had lunched—where he had kissed her—the stream where they had watered their horses.

She stopped to let Arrow drink there again before going on to the beginning of the climb to Hardknott Castle. Hardknott wasn't her destination, just the arbor a much shorter climb up.

After tying Arrow to the very same tree as before, she took from her saddlebags, along with a packet that contained lunch, a pair of stout brogues.

Sitting on the ground to remove her boots, the memories crowded in on her thick and fast.

If you want to try it again one day, we'll start out much earlier, wearing sensible walking shoes.

It was much earlier, her shoes were sensible, but there was no *we* about it. She was alone.

No Roy to laugh with her, no Roy to laugh *at* her, no Roy to admonish or scold, praise or admire, sing bawdy songs or simply to talk with.

It was a hot day, and by the time she reached the clearing where they had spent the night together, she was clammily wet, exhausted, and out of breath. But that was not why she dropped her face in her hands and cried like a heartbroken child.

The arbor—*their* arbor—was gone. Flattened, no doubt, by an autumn storm or a winter snow. All that remained of it now were hundreds of snapped-off branches, dry as kindling, and dozens of long, trailing vines. They were scattered all over the clearing . . . only the long rock slab still marked the spot.

Sinking ankle-deep in scratch branches, Mara walked close to the slab, her hands caressing it. She closed her eyes, remembering the hard rock against her back, sheltering her from the wind behind while his body warmed her in front.

She found a half-cleared spot near a scraggy bush and spread her jacket to sit on. Almost four years since she had been here with Roy. She had been just fifteen then; she would soon be nineteen.

He was two and twenty now, young perhaps, but still of man's age. If he had wanted

her, he would have come back. If his duty
prevented his coming, then he could have
written.

His last communication had been a short
note of condolence when he learned—
probably from Duggie—of Griselda's death.
Before that, nothing for a year. She could
recite his last letter in her sleep, every
damned friendly, brotherly, impersonal word
of it.

He had said in this very spot that he would
be grateful to her all his life. Well, that was
probably true. He had climbed up this path,
tortured by doubts about his manhood, and
he had gone down, all those doubts resolved.

The marriage? Well, no matter how often
she forgot it, Roy wasn't just Roy but Lord
Raleigh Irwine, son of a noble duke. He was
a gentleman and lived by a gentleman's
code. One didn't seduce *or* get seduced by a
girl of good family like Sir Cuthbert Rydale's
fifteen-year-old daughter and not do the right
thing by her.

*Someday, when you're all grown up, if
you still want me to, I'll court you in style
. . . I'm coming back, Mara. No matter how
many years it takes, I'm coming back.*

Ah well, gratitude hadn't driven him quite
so far as that. No doubt it had dimmed
somewhat with the passage of the years.
Mara was glad of that, she told herself,
fiercely, proudly glad. She lifted up her head,
switching the mane of blue-black hair back

and forth disdainfully. She thought too well of herself to want any man out of gratitude.

It had to be the way it had been on this mountain—or not at all!

She had been confident the first year or two after he went away, then less so but still hopeful. Until she was eighteen. Both hope and confidence had died a slow death during this last year.

Girls of his class—*her* class, too, if she had been bred up more like the daughter of Lady Mary Kendal and Sir Cuthbert Rydale—were brought out at the age of eighteen, thrown on the public auction block for marriage, and expected to be speedily off their parents' hands.

He must know that even more surely than she. He must know he courted the danger of losing her. Or did he think that Emma and Angus, who were not in favor of such young marriage, would keep her safe for him till he was ready?

Till *he* was ready. Her pride revolted.

While he adventured in faraway places, was she presumed to be waiting faithfully, patiently in Cumbria like some damned Penelope? Was she to wait till he chose to claim her? *If* he chose to claim her?

Not very likely.

Chapter Twenty

ALL MARA'S WISHING AND WONDERING AND heart-burning and yearning were wasted. Neither Duggie nor Roy came home, after all. Instead, brief unsatisfactory notes arrived from the two of them.

Duggie wrote them all that he had been suffering from a recurrent fever but was nicely recovered now and, unlike so many unlucky devils forced to demobilize, he was fortunate enough to be in expectation of a special assignment to Paris in the train of such staff as Wellington might take there with him. His family was always in his thoughts and P.S., he might get some leave before year's end.

Roy wrote Mara at Rydale that he hadn't wanted to worry them all with details of a wound—seemingly a scratch—suffered at St. Pierre in a mere skirmish the previous December. It had become infected and he had come close to losing a leg but was fine now and off to Paris. He and Duggie would probably be meeting there, and they would drink all the family's health in the best champagne the city of the former emperor had to offer. It didn't look as though he would be getting home this year. With fond remembrances to all at Treeways, he was hers devotedly, Roy.

"Mine devotedly. The hell you are!" said Mara out loud to the shocked astonishment of Patty, her little country maid. She crumpled the letter and threw it aside in a passion, but a moment later she was smoothing out the single sheet and hungrily reading it again.

Gifts arrived from Paris a little late for Donnie's and Mara's nineteenth birthday—a lace fan from Duggie, a gold bracelet from Roy. No letters. If both senders had materialized in front of Mara at the moment Emma handed over their offerings, she would gladly and vigorously have boxed two sets of ears.

Donnie, unbothered by the lack of letters, was overwhelmed to be the possessor of a captured French pistol and a Spanish dress sword.

Revolted by his enthusiasm, Mara walked outside before she gave in to the temptation to box his ears as well.

Sir Cuthbert, home from another of his business journeys, reminded himself belatedly that she had passed her nineteenth birthday while he was gone and gave her a gift too. Her grandmother Rydale's pearls.

"Griselda was very fond of them," he said unemotionally, handing her the velvet case.

"I know," said Mara softly. "Thank you very much, Father. They're lovely."

She hesitated, fearing it would pain him to see the pearls around her throat.

As though he had guessed her thought, he said brusquely, "Put them on, child. Put them on. Pearls should be worn or they lose their luster."

Obediently she clasped the double strand around her neck and went over to a mirror to admire the effect.

"Nineteen," she heard her father say behind her. "It hardly seems possible. A girl should be settled by nineteen. It's time I was thinking of your marriage."

Mara spun around. "Thank you, sir, but I have no wish to be settled. I am content with my life as it is."

"Nonsense. You must be married one day. What other life can there be for a woman?"

"Unfortunately, very little. I *will* marry one day, Father, when I feel so inclined, but there's no great hurry. Marriage," she reminded him shrewdly, "lasts a long, long time, and we cannot all expect to be as fortunate in the union chosen as you and Griselda were."

He gave a short, pleased bark of laughter.

"No, to be sure most are not. But Griselda . . . a fine woman, my Griselda. She was someone special."

"Well, then, Father, permit me to find someone special too."

"That's a father's duty, my dear."

"Did *her* father perform that duty for *my* mother?" Mara asked him sharply, knowing as soon as the words tumbled off her unruly tongue that she had blundered sadly and by this bit of impertinence lost all the ground she might have gained.

Sir Cuthbert eyed her coldly. "You're the mistress of Rydale, miss, not a farmer's daughter from Treeways. I have been presuming that you knew how to behave like a lady. If I was mistaken, perhaps it is time your connection with the MacTavishes was ended."

Subduing both her fright and her temper, Mara offered profuse apologies. Her father appeared to accept these unreservedly, but immediately after that unfortunate exchange, she noticed a tendency on his part to curtail her visits to Emma.

He never actually forbade her to go to Treeways, but he would frequently find something else he wanted her to do when she planned to go there. Or even when she only wanted to ride out alone.

He would like her to ride out with him, he would suggest, smiling; it was time she learned the affairs of the estate that would one day be hers. Or he expressed a sudden desire for her company into Carlisle to the office of Mr. Firkin. Another time the excuse was that the Dowlings and Firths were expected to call; it was time she became better acquainted with the neighboring gentry.

Knowing that she had brought this on herself, for several months Mara yielded with every appearance of patience and good will. She spoke softly and stepped quietly, biding her time, and was finally rewarded by permission to go to the Cottage when Sir Cuthbert went away on his next journey in January of 1815.

Mara sent one of the grooms to Treeways with a note that she would be coming in two days' time. It was raining hard on the morning her father left, but she was too impatient to delay. Ordering Arrow to be brought to her whenever the weather improved, she had one of the grooms drive her over in Griselda's light lady's carriage.

When the carriage stopped in front of the cottage, Donnie came down the steps of the veranda to meet her, half hidden by the big old umbrella kept in the hallway. The carriage door was opened and a hand held out to her.

"Thank you, Donnie love," said Mara, bunching up her skirts and jumping down, avoiding a puddle.

"Donnie love, indeed," said a laughing, loving voice as the hand pulled her under the umbrella and then against a hard, broader, sturdier chest than Donnie's.

"Duggie, oh, Duggie." She flung her arms around him and sobbed against his neck.

"Hey, you're drowning me, Merry," he said after a while, holding her tightly and balancing the umbrella over them at the same time. "And we're both drowning out here. Why not go into the house where you can cry comfortably?"

"Oh, you!" said Mara, but she went up the steps with him, not letting go her fierce grip even when he bent to lay the umbrella on the veranda to dry and opened the front door.

"It's the most wonderful surprise that ever was. When did you get here?" she asked happily, wiping her feet before she stepped into Emma's clean hallway.

"Yesterday morning."

"Yesterday." She looked up at him reproachfully.

"I know, Merry, but Mam agreed with me that it would be better for your big brother"— he grinned lazily down at her—"not to go to Rydale, and I knew you would be coming here today."

"Have you seen Roy lately?" She kept her face carefully hidden as she asked the hopeful question.

"Not for a couple of months. I may meet him in Paris in March."

"Is that when you have to go back?"

203

"The end of February."

She winked back fresh tears, telling herself they were still for Duggie. "Less than two months after three years away."

"It's better than nothing, Mara. Look at poor Roy."

"Poor Roy, indeed! I'm sure if a duke's son really wanted leave, it would be his for the asking. 'Poor Roy' is probably having a marvelous time for himself."

"Well," admitted Duggie cautiously, his attention caught by a certain something in her voice, "Roy would be the last to deny that he *is* challenged by the work, but I know first-hand that he's a splendid soldier and perhaps being a duke's son *has* given him a strong sense of duty."

"Men and their duty," sniffed Mara, thinking of her father and his last use of that word as well as of Roy and of Duggie. "Have you ever noticed how frequently their duty is in accord with their desires?"

Duggie laughed as they both went into the parlor, where the family was gathered.

"Listen to her." He winked across at Angus. "Five minutes ago she was weeping all over my shoulder, supposedly with joy at my homecoming. And already the little shrew is nagging me. God pity her husband."

Mara smiled impishly as she kissed Emma and Angus, then Nurse. "God had better," she informed them, "because I won't."

Donnie came in from the barn on a scene of loud hilarity and had to be told the cause.

"Husband!" he scoffed to Mara. "Who'd have you? Men want to come home to peace and quiet, not constant brangles."

"And good food," Mara reminded him, pinching one plump cheek and then his belly. "You forget I'm a good cook. If I find someone like *you*, that may be more important than a sweet disposition."

They all laughed again, as though she had said something incredibly witty. They would have laughed at anything, they were all so full of joy.

It was the merriest, happiest week that Mara, as well as the MacTavishes, had known for a very long time. On the eighth day, when her father's summons came, her heart rebelled angrily.

"I don't want to go!" she stormed to Emma, who looked at her with troubled eyes and reminded her, "You *must* go, Mara, lass."

Mara burst into tears. "I hate being a girl!" she sobbed. "I hate being made to feel helpless. I'm tired of men running my life."

"Mara, Mara," Emma sighed, "why must you always go charging at life head-first instead of using what's inside it?"

Mara blew her nose hard into a lace handkerchief. "What does that mean?" she sniffled.

"You know that you can get around your father if you use tact and sense instead of being mule-headed. Go home, be obedient, be pleasant, and after a few days ask sweetly —*ask,* not demand, mind you—if he can spare you to spend a little time with your dear-loved brother before he goes back to foreign parts. And no sarcasm when you speak of your brother, miss. Remember to use treacle, not vinegar."

"Games," Mara said scornfully.

"Aye, games that help to get a woman what she wants in a man's world."

"It's demeaning," Mara said accusingly. "Do you have to do that with Da?"

Emma laughed deep in her throat. "As little as any woman in the world, I'd say," she acknowledged, a strange smile still lingering on her lips. "But then my man is no ordinary man, while *your* father is master of Rydale, accustomed to having his wishes and orders obeyed. You can fight him and butt your head against a stone wall, or you can seem docile but wily and get your own way."

"Oh, very well." Mara's hair slapped violently against her shoulders. "But the man *I* marry," she warned pettishly, "will be like Da. I am dam—*defi*nitely not going to spend my life playing games."

"I doubt that the man with the courage to marry *you,* lassie," said Emma, eyes twinkling, "will have any need to play them."

Mara tried to look indignant but wound up bursting out laughing even as her thoughts returned wistfully to Roy. With Roy she had been herself.

She would have been astonished to know that Emma's mind was traveling the same road. How she wanted Lord Raleigh Irwine for this beloved child, though not because he *was* Lord Raleigh Irwine. She wanted Mara to have Duggie's Roy. Prankster Roy of Eton. The Roy who had learned to milk cows, mow hay, and plow. The Roy who ate her pies like a greedy schoolboy. The hurt Roy, the vulnerable Roy; the madcap but manly boy who understood her Mara.

In the wildest dreams and worst nightmares of the two, neither would have believed that Mara's future husband, chosen by Sir Cuthbert, was waiting to meet his bride when she returned to Rydale. The latest of Sir Cuthbert's "business" trips had borne sweet ripe fruit. He had found the very man he was seeking.

There had been close to a dozen names on his original list when Mr. Firkin was done with an investigation. Three had to be weeded out immediately; they were seven, ten, and eleven. Not only were they too young for his strong-willed daughter; Sir Cuthbert could not afford to wait for nursery children to grow up.

Four others of the right age, most regrettably, already had wives. One gentleman who suited him perfectly had inherited wealth and estates from his own father and did not need to exchange his rightful name in order to gain more. Another, *almost* a gentleman, was poor but unaccountably proud; he stubbornly persisted in a preference for his own name.

Two men were left on the list. Julian Carleton was a twenty-five-year-old Londoner who was discovered to be a drunkard, a gambler, a wastrel, a womanizer. Obviously, he would not do at all for Rydale!

Carleton's name was crossed out by Sir Cuthbert without so much as an initial visit, leaving Nestor Gray-Gordon of York in sole possession of the field. *Not yet twenty, only son of Lydia Gray-Gordon, your father's eldest niece,* was noted after his name in Mr. Firkin's small, precise hand.

It might have been as well for Mara to have a husband a few years older than she, stubborn puss that she was. On the other hand, for Sir Cuthbert's purpose, a nineteen-year-old might be more desirable. He was more likely to be malleable; Sir Cuthbert could train him in the way he wanted. Mara and this boy could grow up together, the father assured himself on his way to pay a visit of ceremony, having sent a formal announcement of his intent the night before.

As soon as he set eyes on Nestor Gray-Gordon, Sir Cuthbert was satisfied that he had found the right husband for Mara. The fellow was almost indecently handsome in the way made fashionable by that rackety fellow Byron.

He had a tall lean figure, broad, unpadded shoulders, flat stomach, and a good leg. His fine-chiseled, somewhat haughty profile was framed by a mop of dark curls almost as black as Mara's own straight thick hair.

The girl was bound to be attracted to him; girls her age, he knew, were highly suscepti-ble to such extreme good looks. It was obvi-ous the boy's own mother doted on him fondly.

Spoiled him, too, no doubt, decided Sir Cuthbert, his shrewdness not altogether de-serting him in spite of a strong inclination to get the matter settled. Well, all the better. Gray-Gordon had been taught his own worth and doubtless had every intention of better-ing his condition through marriage.

If he was ambitious—and he struck the baronet as an ambitious, self-serving sort of fellow—he wanted a great deal more out of life than a widowed mother of limited means could provide for him.

A few cautious questions elicited the infor-mation that there was no prior betrothal to make further negotiations useless.

Sir Cuthbert extended a private invitation to young Nestor Gray-Gordon to dine with him at his inn that night. Nestor accepted readily, having developed very young a sixth sense for situations that might be to his advantage.

During the course of dinner, the host was unsurprised to confirm a strong suspicion that his guest was a fiercely ambitious young man with no great attachment to his father's name—not if it stood in the way of his advancement. He would gladly discard Gray-Gordon and become a Rydale—provided it profited him.

When Sir Cuthbert left York a few days later to return to Rydale Park, Nestor (temporarily Gray-Gordon) shared his carriage, and the two had come to a tolerable understanding.

Chapter Twenty-one

SIR CUTHBERT WOULD HAVE BEEN DISMAYED to know that his daughter took an almost instant dislike to the protégé he brought home to be her husband. As mistress of Rydale and his hostess—also, keeping in mind Emma's late lecture—Mara was scrupulously polite to her newly acquired "Cousin Nestor." No onlooker could have known that she was repelled by everything about the unwanted guest from his obsequious manners and smooth compliments to his Byronic curls and profile. She mistrusted his too-ready charm.

Her first impressions were ineradicable. Reared in an atmosphere of warmth and spontaneity, with brothers who were frank, honest, open, even sometimes disagreeably outspoken, Mara had always preferred those who spoke their minds; who, even at the risk of being awkward or saying a wrong thing, were direct, candid, and sincere.

Nestor Gray-Gordon was anything, *every*-thing but candid and sincere. He spoke only to please and he judged her so little intelligent that she would be unaware of the true value of the honeyed phrases that tripped so readily off his tongue whenever he addressed her.

A week after his arrival, bored by her cousin's company and bothered by his ever-hovering presence, Mara delayed going to Mrs. Bostwick one morning in order to seek out her father in the library.

"When is Nestor going home, sir?" she asked him baldly, leaving off the courtesy "cousin."

"He will probably stay the winter." Sir Cuthbert eyed her warily, knowing when she groaned out loud that he must tread easy. A great pity that she had not succumbed as readily as he had hoped.

"Why are you disappointed, Mara? Your cousin, in general, appears to have the power to please, and he is undoubtedly much struck by you."

"That young man," said Mara disdainfully, "is struck by no one but himself. What makes his company so wearing is the way he tries so hard to ingratiate himself with me."

Her voice changed suddenly, becoming softly sweet, almost meek. "Father, I have been meaning to ask you, may I return to Treeways? My brother is returned from the Continent on leave from the army, but he has to go back in another month; and after three years' absence I should like to spend as much time with him as I am able."

His first impulse was to refuse out of hand on the grounds that it would be rude to their guest. Just in time he realized that the independent chit would just grow more stubborn if he refused her. He was cursing his own lack of foresight, as he gave bland consent, in permitting her to be raised at Treeways. She should never have been allowed to be shaped so much out of the proper conventional mold.

"I would suggest, however, that you wait a few days before you go," he added with a casual air. "I should not like your cousin to feel you were running away so rudely the moment he arrives."

Pleased to have won the greater point, Mara felt she could afford to give way on the minor. It was this kind of conciliation, she knew, that Emma had tried so hard to teach her.

Back at Treeways, Mara enlivened their first meal together with her mimicry of Nestor Gray-Gordon.

Miss Mara, your smile brightens the day and shames the sun.

My dear Miss Mara, you are far lovelier

than the roses. See how they wither in your presence.

Sweet cousin, will you play and sing for me? Though just your voice is music to the ears.

Donnie made a retching sound, which he hastily turned into a cough when Angus gave him a look.

Duggie asked lazily, "How do you answer him?"

Cousin Nestor, the sun doesn't shine when it rains.

Dear Cousin Nestor, I fear that what has withered the roses is too little water, not too much me.

It would not be sweet, cousin, if I played and sang for you. I fear I have no aptitude for music.

Everyone enjoyed a good laugh except Emma, who sat looking thoughtful. When the men went outdoors for evening chores and Nurse was settled in a rocker with her knitting, she said to Mara as they prepared the next day's bread dough, "Why do you suppose your father invited yon cousin to Rydale?"

"Oh, I suppose—" Mara stopped, all at once struck by the same horrid thought as Emma. "You don't *really* suppose," she asked in consternation, "that Sir Cuthbert thinks I would ever be willing to accept that pretty popinjay?"

"I can't say what's in Sir Cuthbert's mind," answered Emma cautiously, "but best keep it in mind, my girl."

Mara went back to Rydale five days later, certain that Mam, usually infallible, must surely be wrong this time. After a few days, as she studied her father's manner and listened to Cousin Nestor's more cautious compliments—Sir Cuthbert had advised him not to be so fulsome—she was not so positive.

She sought out her father in the library again.

"Sir, why did you invite Nestor here?" she asked him bluntly.

"He is a family connection," he pointed out quite gently.

"The only times I have ever seen any family connections here at Rydale," said Mara, with her deplorable MacTavish frankness, "were at my mother's funeral, and at Griselda's."

There was nothing to be gained by fencing with her; he knew his daughter too well by now to believe she would drop her guard.

"Your cousin Nestor," Sir Cuthbert told her in a voice that chilled her with its quiet certainty, "is the only family connection eligible to be your husband. He is also willing to change his name back to Rydale."

"Back?"

"On the female side, he is a Rydale. It would be proper for him to take the name when he marries you and becomes future master here."

Mara drew a deep breath. "Father, he can become future master here with my good will, if that's what you intend. But he doesn't have to marry me to do it. In fact, he won't . . . because I shan't have him."

"Would you rather lose Rydale? Would you rather live on what Griselda left you than be the greatest heiress in the county?"

"Yes," said Mara, looking him straight in the eye. "I think I would, if that's what it would mean. You see, I don't even like him."

"At nineteen a girl's head is often filled with rubbishing thoughts of romance, and she is ready to dismiss the comforts and elegancies of life she longs for later. Fortunately, fathers exist to save such silly misses from themselves. One day, when you are truly mistress of Rydale, you will thank me for not having taken you seriously now."

"Haven't you listened to me at all, Father?"

"Haven't you listened to *me*, daughter? I am not asking you, I am exerting a father's *authority* to tell you. You will marry Nestor Gray-Gordon, and you may have the rest of the winter to become accustomed to that fact. We will announce the betrothal at a grand ball in the spring, when our year's mourning is over. The wedding will take place in the summer, by which time the legalities of his name change will be completed."

Mara subdued her first impulse to rail wildly at him, to deny that she would do any such thing. Her father's eyes glittered so strangely in his pale face; his mouth twisted as he issued his cold instructions. Even his hands . . . they were shaking in the palsied fashion of an old, old man. He frightened her.

"You will honeymoon here under our own roof," Sir Cuthbert continued, looking up as though he were addressing God rather than his daughter, "and my grandsons will be born Rydales."

He directed his glittering glance back to Mara. "Do you understand me?" he asked her in a hard, implacable voice.

With the greatest exertion of will she had ever shown—how proud Mam would be of her when she heard!—Mara answered in a quiet, colorless voice that was utterly unlike her. "Yes, Father, I understand."

Sir Cuthbert peered at her, not entirely disarmed. "And you will behave properly?"

"Yes, Father," Mara lied humbly. "I will behave properly," she added with a low cunning that she thought might further lull his suspicion. "In the marriage settlements, you will protect me, won't you, so he doesn't have control of all the money? I want something that's my own the way that Griselda did."

"I shall assure you a handsome independent jointure." Sir Cuthbert smiled in relief. "Nestor is in no position to object to any demands or restrictions I make," he added with careless honesty. "Never fear, the settlements will be drawn up by Firkin, according to my instructions, and you will be the most envied bride that ever walked down the aisle."

Half to lend credence to her charade and half out of genuine curiosity, Mara asked another hesitant question. "Suppose I don't have any children?"

Her father looked at her with blankly uncomprehending eyes.

"Sup-pose"—she was almost afraid to continue—"suppose I—I can't."

Sir Cuthbert smote the desk again and again with clenched fist. "You will have them!" he shouted at her. "You will." Then once more he looked upward. "I *must* have grandsons." He seemed to be addressing God again. Mara sat very still till he was done haranguing the Almighty.

"Go," he told her then. "Send Handley to me with some wine. But remember what I said."

Mara stood up and dropped a respectful curtsy. "Yes, Father," she said dutifully.

Exerting even greater strength than she had shown in the confrontation with her father, Mara made no mention of returning to Treeways till nine days had passed. She wanted to make sure that he would not think she was rushing there to demand protection from the ultimatum he had given her.

It was exactly what she intended to do, of course, but at a time and in a way that would not give away her intention to frustrate his plans.

She arrived at the cottage on a windy February day. One look at her face and Angus asked, "What's troubling you, lass?"

"Mam was right," said Mara in a trembly voice, not aware till now, when she felt safe and secure, how very frightened she had been these last nine days at Rydale. "Sir Cuthbert intends me to marry Nestor Gray-Gordon, who will change his name to Rydale. Then *I* will be used to breed lots of little Rydales."

"Did you talk to him? Did you tell him how you feel?" Angus pursued, and Emma as well as Mara shook her head.

"He doesn't want to talk, especially about how *I* feel. He only knows how *he* feels. I can't talk to him." Mara shivered a little. "He scares me," she confessed. "He sounds —well, almost crazed when he talks about my giving him sons for Rydale. He always was—a little about that, I think—but with Griselda he became more human."

"It's all he has now, poor man," Emma said compassionately.

"Poor man!" Mara repeated indignantly. "How about me? He's quite prepared to sacrifice *me*."

"I feel sorry for your father, Mara, indeed I do, which doesn't mean I won't oppose him with my last breath. Not that I think 'twill be necessary. I'm sure that you've already hatched your own plot."

A smile broke through the trouble on Mara's face. "You can always outguess us all, Mam. Of course I have. I'm going to go with Duggie when he leaves."

Pandemonium broke out in the Treeways parlor, Duggie and Donnie and Angus maintaining that she would do no such thing and Mara maintaining that if Duggie didn't take her then she would go by herself.

Emma dropped a quiet question into the middle of the uproar.

"Why shouldn't she go?" she asked her menfolk. "I think the time is right for her to leave here."

Her menfolk stared back at her in astonished disbelief, while Mara crowed in triumph. Then they all started shouting at once.

"You don't mean that you'd abet her in any such wild scheme, lass!"

"Sir Cuthbert would make an almighty stink, Mam!"

"For God's sakes, Mam, do you expect me to take her with me to war?"

"There is no war now, Duggie, remember?

I'll just go to whatever country you're going to be in, and you can set me up in lodgings. I'll hire a maid to be with me for respectability, if you think it's needful, Mam—"

Emma nodded.

"It won't be forever, just till I'm one and twenty and my father has no say over me. Then I'll have an income of two hundred pounds or more from the rent of Griselda's house in London. And by the time I'm four and twenty, I'll have my inheritance from her, so it won't matter if Sir Cuthbert disinherits me."

"What will you travel and live on till then? I'll share whatever I have, Mara, but God knows an officer's pay hardly covers his own expenses—unless he has a private income—and you would need much more than I to be established comfortably."

"I have more than one hundred pounds put by now," Mara said, "and tomorrow—no, this afternoon, I shall go into Carlisle to see Mr. Firkin and ask, in confidence, if he will advance me anything on my inheritance. If not, I can work, can't I, Duggie? I'd want to, anyhow. I could be governess to an officer's children. I could teach French to the English or English to the French. I can cook, I can nurse . . . and it will be for less than two years. Stop worrying; it's going to be the grandest adventure of my life."

The three men were no match for the united front presented by the women of the family. Once they could be made to see that the threat to Mara was serious, they lost all real desire to oppose her.

It became a question of how to get her away.

"When did your father bid you home, lass?" Emma asked her.

"Friday a week."

She turned to Duggie. "And when must you take leave of us?" she asked her son.

"In about a se'nnight, Mam."

"Then there's no time to be lost," said Emma, lips tight set. "Mara is right; she had better go into Carlisle this very afternoon to see Mr. Firkin. And the two of you should take off tomorrow."

They all gaped at her.

"Did you expect the girl to go home and announce to her father that she's planning to run away?" demanded Emma impatiently. "The more time there is before he starts chasing after her, the better. Leave a letter to him here with me, Mara. I'll send it on whatever day he was expecting you. By then he'll have no hope of catching up."

Duggie gave a great shout of laughter and lifted her right off her feet. "You should have been a general, Mam. We'd have beat Boney years ago."

Mara said longingly, "It would mean your losing six days of Duggie's visit."

Angus spoke up. "Whist, Mara lass, you're fighting for your whole life; we'll not begrudge six days of our Duggie's time." He put one hand on his wife's shoulder as he spoke, and she looked up at him with clear, loving eyes. Her hand went up to touch his.

It was Mara, not Emma, who began to cry. "I love you all so much," she sobbed. "When I'm one and twenty and my father can't order my life, I shall come home to you at Treeways."

Chapter Twenty-two

In London, Duggie found that his orders had been changed. He was forced to cool his heels for several weeks, during which Mara hid out in Kensington with a friend from Miss Petersham's seminary. It was late March before the two of them took ship across the Channel for Ostend and from there traveled by coach the seventy miles to Brussels.

Duggie had barely gotten her established in a room in the Hotel de Belle-Vue on the Palais Royale and was looking around for more permanent lodgings, preferably with some respectable lady, when he found himself ordered back to Ostend.

He had only time to buy a horse and rush to the hotel to bid Mara good-bye, begging her at the same time to please, for God's sakes, stay out of trouble.

"Just what," she asked him, eyes dancing, "do you think I'm proposing to do in your absence?"

"That's what will turn my hair white while I'm away." Duggie groaned. "Please get yourself a chaperone. I left word for Roy at headquarters, in case he turns up, to look after you."

Seeing his genuine worry, Mara bit back the temptation to snap that she didn't need any help from Roy.

"I'll try to get lodgings with some older woman," she promised, "and if I remove, I'll leave word at the desk where I can be found."

In mid-April Duggie returned to Brussels and, on inquiring at the desk, was told that yes, Miss Rydale was still with them but she had driven out, as she did early every morning, in her donkey cart.

"Oh, God!" Duggie groaned, tugging at his hair. "Where does she go? When does she get back?"

"I don't know, Lieutenant, but you need have no fears for the young lady's safety. As I was just telling the other gentleman, she returns early each evening under the escort of two of your fine English soldiers."

Duggie looked about him. "Which other gentleman?"

"The captain—there he is in the blue uniform, just going out the door."

Duggie looked toward the door and gave a great shout. "Roy!"

The next moment they were blocking the entrance as they stood pounding and pummeling each other, both demanding together, "When did you get in? Do you know where Mara is?"

Duggie threw up his hands, and Roy grinned. "Driving out in a donkey cart. Where the hell do you suppose she goes?"

"Well, I need a meal, a bath, and a change of clothes, so my curiosity will have to wait till early evening. Come along, I want to know all about your doings since France."

"*Mañana*," said Roy, coloring slightly. "*My* curiosity won't wait. I'm going searching."

Duggie raised his eyebrows. "Oh?"

It was Roy's turn to shrug. "I haven't seen the girl for four and a half years. Has she . . . is she . . . Never mind, I'll find out for myself soon enough." He unbuttoned his jacket and pulled a flat packet from inside it. "Will you stop by at headquarters and deliver these for me? I want to get started now. Let's meet back here at eight, and the three of us can dine together at the Tivoli."

Duggie took the packet and executed a mock-formal salute. "Eight o'clock it is, sir."

Roy had already discovered from the doorman at the hotel the direction of the stable where Mara rented her donkey cart. The first groom he spoke to at the stable was prompt to answer his question about Miss Rydale. It appeared that every groom at the stable was acquainted with the *belle* English lady who drove the donkey cart daily to Grammont.

Roy rode swiftly out of Brussels toward the nearby village of Grammont. On the outskirts he stopped to make some inquiries of a Belgian peasant couple, who responded with blank stares; a group of three British soldiers was more forthcoming.

"Would you be meaning the little lady with the face of an angel, the voice of a choirboy, and the hair black as midnight that she wears loike the tail of a horse?" an Irish corporal inquired poetically.

Lord Raleigh Irwine laughed aloud in pleasure and relief.

"I can't think of a better description of Miss Mara Rydale," he said buoyantly.

"Right down the road, sir, the way you're headed, then take the first left turn. There's a barn there just beyond a row of three houses where they've set up school."

"School."

"She's the teacher, sir," a private offered.

"The teacher. Of course. What else? My thanks, men. Buy yourselves an ale."

The corporal deftly caught the coin that was tossed, and a grateful chorus of thanks followed Roy as he galloped on down the road.

At the barn there were at least twenty children of both sexes and assorted sizes, but no Mara. The middle-aged woman who was trying to keep order explained over the head of the small boy wriggling on her lap that Miss Rydale had been sent for two hours ago to help with Mrs. Mercer's baby.

"I beg your pardon."

"Mrs. Mercer's baby was about to be born"—the matron enunciated her explanation slowly and patiently as though Roy were about the age of the two-year-old on her lap—"so naturally they sent for Miss Rydale."

"Naturally," Roy echoed, dazed. "Er—ma'am, could you direct me to Mrs. Mercer's?"

"Continue on the Grammont road for about a half-mile till you see two houses almost opposite one another; it's the one on the right."

When he got to the house described, he tied his horse at the fence and knocked vigorously at the door. No one answered. He knocked again and then walked in just as a woman's piercing scream shattered the air.

It was painfully reminiscent of sounds heard during the war in Spain, when the conquering soldiery, battle-mad and out of hand, swarmed over a village after the fighting was done.

"Mara!" He took the steps two at a time.

Halfway up, he heard a baby's cry and,

feeling rather foolish, stopped on the landing while his pounding heart returned to normal.

A little circle of women collected in the upstairs hallway directed their curious stares at him.

"Captain Mercer?" asked one.

"No, sorry. I'm Captain Irwine."

"Oh." They continued to whisper among themselves while they waited. Roy stood silently.

Presently a door opened and Mara walked out, holding a small bundle in her arms.

"It's a girl," said the well-remembered "voice of a choirboy" as the other women gathered round her with exclamations of delight. The bundle must have been handed over to one of them, because when Mara broke away from the group, her arms were hanging tiredly at her sides. Beads of sweat, which no lady was ever supposed to acquire, covered her shiny face from forehead to chin. The big apron she wore over her flowered muslin dress was spotted with blood.

In spite of her obvious fatigue, her eyes were sparklingly bright and she was smiling a secret smile. She jauntily flipped the mane of blue-black hair over her shoulders as she approached the stairs.

"Mara," he said.

Her eyes widened in shock. "Roy?" It seemed almost a question. She took one tentative step down. "You're—older. You've—changed."

He took three steps up. "You haven't, my beautiful girl."

Blood and sweat and all, he took her into his arms.

The women above riveted their eyes on the romantic embrace taking place below; their eyes misted over in sentimental sympathy. When the couple drew apart, they screeched in shock to see Miss Rydale's arm flash high just before her palm dealt the man she had kissed so passionately a resounding slap across the cheek.

Roy, still reeling from the kiss, was nearly knocked off his feet by the slap.

"What the hell was that for?" he shouted furiously.

"I promised myself to do that the very first chance I got!" Mara shouted right back. "It's for all the letters you never wrote and all the leaves you never took and all the—all the—"

"I've a good mind to give you a taste of the same." But even as he said it and the imprint of her fingers showed redder on his face, he took her back into his arms and kissed her till he felt her tears rolling down both their cheeks.

"Let's go outside, darling, but better take off that apron first."

She untied the bloodstained apron and tossed it across the newel post at the bottom of the stairs.

Seated on the grass near the fence where Roy had tied his horse, she looked anywhere but at him. "Did you *really* deliver that baby?" he wanted to know.

"Not by myself, but I assisted the doctor."

"Where in the world did you learn how to assist?"

"A physician in Bath taught me. I can set bones, too, and sew cuts and nurse a fever," she stated proudly.

"I suppose it would be too much to ask"—his voice was suspiciously meek and humble—"just how and why a physician in Bath should have taught you all these lady-of-fashion skills."

Mara's head lifted high; predictably, the mane of hair went slap-slap against her shoulders. "Because *I* asked him to! I thought they would be *useful* skills."

"Useful how—and where?"

"Here. Wherever an army goes. You know, I always wanted to follow the drum."

"Yes, I seem to remember—with Duggie. I thought, perhaps, over the years you had changed your mind."

"Not really. It just didn't seem likely that . . . but when the chance presented itself . . . and since I had no choice when I had to get out of England, I—"

"Wait a minute. What was that? Why did you *have* to get out of England?"

"My father was trying to force me to marry a perfectly detestable cousin of mine, who was willing to change his name to Rydale. Sir Cuthbert was—well, ever since Griselda died he's been crackbrained on the subject of my having sons for Rydale. So I ran away," she finished rather defiantly.

She took a quick look up at Roy, who sat with his hands clenched over his knees and his set face staring frowningly ahead.

"I suppose," she challenged him defiantly, "you think it wasn't proper behavior for me, *Lord Raleigh.*"

His face softened into amusement as he stared at her haughty profile. "Now, *that* piece of impertinence, Miss Rydale," he told her mildly, "does rather deserve a return slap."

He laughed as her eyes dared him.

After a minute he reminded her lightly, "I'm hardly in a position to cavil at your running away. Or is your memory so much shorter than mine you've forgotten that I once ran away with you myself?"

"I have a very good memory, Lord Ra—Roy," she substituted hastily. "*I* forget nothing."

I'm coming back, Mara. No matter how many years it takes, I'm coming back.

"What is that supposed to mean?"

Her lips trembled. If he didn't know, she wasn't about to tell him.

"Duggie didn't want to bring me at first," she explained hastily for a change of subject, "but Mam insisted that he should."

His ears perked up. *"Mam?"*

"Yes." She forgot to be formal and distancing for a moment. "I must admit I was surprised as anyone when she said it was the right time for me to follow the army."

"Mam said *that*?"

"Yes, exactly that. So, of course, when *she* agreed with me, they all agreed."

"Of course. But what I don't understand" —his voice became carefully expressionless —"is why you and Duggie didn't think of . . . of marrying in England."

Mara bent her head, very absorbed in the study of two blades of grass she had just plucked from the earth. She felt as though she had been dealt a much harder blow than the slap she had given Roy.

"There wasn't any question of us—our marrying." The calm words were forced from out of a dry throat. She felt sick inside. "Duggie—you *know*, we were brought up brother and sister. He never felt—about me— like that. But, of course, he was willing to look after me."

Roy nodded his head, one opinion confirmed. He felt only a partial lifting of his heart as he asked her, "Does your father know where you are, Mara?"

"I didn't tell him in the letter I left, but he's not a stupid man. Since Duggie and I disappeared together, he's bound to suspect I've gone with him."

"Which means all he has to do is discover Duggie's whereabouts from the War Office, and he will be able to make a more-or-less accurate guess about where you are. And another matter—it won't do your reputation any good for it to be known you came off with Duggie. Unchaperoned, I suppose?"

"Utterly, shockingly *un*chaperoned," Mara returned flippantly. "Just as I was when I went up to Hardknott Castle with you, and again at Gretna Green."

Roy flushed. "No one knew about that," he persisted, "but by the time your father's been to the War Office, *everyone* will have heard about this . . . first in England, then Brussels. Gossip travels faster here than the cavalry."

"I don't care."

"Well, you should care, you little fool. Don't you see—not only by going with Duggie, but you with your donkey cart and schoolteaching and doctoring, you've left a wide-open trail for Sir Cuthbert to follow?"

Mara turned deathly white. "He wouldn't. He *couldn't*." She clutched at his sleeve. "We're in Belgium. Roy, he couldn't force me to go back to England, could he?"

"Mara, use your head; he would act through the military. If the British military suggested to the Brussels authorities that you should be returned to your father's care, do you think Belgium would fight your battle?"

"Then much as I don't want to, I'll leave the army," said Mara, almost numb with despair. "I'll change my name if I have to and go away. But I'm *not* going home to marry Nestor Gray-Gordon."

"You don't have to leave the army, and you're certainly not going home to marry Nestor whatever, but I think it would be a good idea to change your name."

"You do?"

"Yes," said Roy, bending over to lightly kiss her mouth. "I do. Lady Roy Irwine sounds right to me."

"Oh?"

"It was your name once before, remember?"

"I rather thought I remembered better than you."

"Glad to hear it," said Roy, unabashed. "Especially since we've been betrothed since you were thirteen, going on fourteen."

"We've been no such thing; you're as crackbrained as my father."

"And you boasting about your memory," he gibed. "We've been betrothed since my first summer at Treeways when you asked me if a duke's son could marry a baronet's daughter and declined to slobber over me on the grounds that men plant the seeds but girls get the babies."

Mara said primly, "It's very kind of you, but I wouldn't dream of forcing you to honor such a long-ago obligation."

Roy heaved a deep sigh. "You haven't changed in one other respect," he told her. "Stubborn as ever. Let us understand one another, Miss Rydale." He bent to lift her from the grass onto his lap. "I've wanted you since you were short of thirteen. I *had* you," he reminded her with embarrassing frankness, "when you were almost fifteen."

Mara tried to lower her crimson face but wasn't permitted to.

"To be even more blunt, dear girl, three times on a mountain only whetted *my* appetite . . . and since *you* need a husband both to save your reputation and to protect you from your father, marriage seems the best solution."

"But—" began Mara, even as she prayed her racing heart would not betray her.

"No buts," interrupted Lord Raleigh Irwine. "You'll either marry me, Mara Rydale, or I'll send you back myself to Nestor what's-his-name."

Chapter Twenty-three

MARA'S FEEBLE OBJECTIONS WERE SWEPT aside during the ride back to Brussels. They were not even listened to when she and Roy and Duggie had their dinner at the Tivoli.

Having summed up the facts with military precision, "There is no choice in the matter," the captain informed the lieutenant. "If she doesn't want to be shipped home to England to be married to this Byronic cousin, the chit needs a husband right here in Brussels. I'm willing. Are you?" he challenged.

Duggie's glance at the prospective bride was brimming with malice and mischief. "God forbid!" he uttered piously. "It would take a more heroic man than I . . . one of Nosey's more daring aides, perhaps"—Roy frowned warningly at him—"to take on my 'sweet sister' for life."

"Then it's settled. I'll track down a parson

—even a priest if need be—and make the arrangements."

"I'll give the bride away," volunteered Duggie.

Mara said in a deceptively dulcet voice, "Isn't anyone going to ask for my opinion?"

"No!" they both shot back at her.

Mara began to giggle a little hysterically, and in a few minutes all three of them were drawing the attention of nearby diners by their near-riotous laughter.

The next practical question came from Duggie.

"How soon do you plan the wedding?"

Mara opened her mouth and once more was not given the chance to speak.

"The sooner the better," Roy said promptly, "in case Sir Cuthbert has already contacted the War Office. Besides which, I may have to leave Brussels soon again, so it's best we tie the knot before I do."

"Leave Brussels?" Mara sat up straight, biting her lower lip. "Why? Where would you go?"

"Not so very far," Roy answered lightly. "I'm one of Wellington's minor messenger boys, you know. He keeps me tracking up and down the country delivering notes . . . some of his billets-doux, I wouldn't be surprised."

This ploy succeeded admirably. "Is he really the ladies' man I've heard?" asked Mara, her attention momentarily diverted.

"That depends on what you've heard," Roy answered tantalizingly.

"That he's as mighty in the boudoir as on the battlefield."

"I have no first-hand knowledge of his prowess," murmured the duke's officer, a wicked sparkle in his eye. "I can confirm, however, that he's to be found in one as often as on the other."

"Children, children," complained Duggie. "As a lowly lieutenant, unaccustomed to associating with the nobility or the about-to-be-noble, I find you lacking in respect toward our esteemed commander. "Now, about this wedding—"

"This wedding," said Roy tersely, "will be arranged as expeditiously as possible, and you will be the first informed when it is coming off."

"He'll be the first?" asked Mara with an innocent dagger-sweet smile at her husband-to-be.

"After you, my love, after you," he hastened to amend.

Two days later Mara returned from her schoolteaching in Grammont to discover that her belongings had been moved from her hotel room to a private house in one of the more desirable situations in Brussels, the Rue de la Montagne on the park. She had a suite of elegant rooms, up four stories, in the home of the widowed Comtesse de Lannier.

When Roy came to call, while a maid was

still unpacking her clothes, he found her kneeling on a window seat, watching the parade of Belgians and British in the park.

He came up behind her and pressed his hands on her shoulders, watching, too, for a moment. "It's like Hyde Park at the fashionable hour," he said casually. "I sometimes think half the ton of London has bought seats for a war the way they do for the opera."

"Well, at least half the matchmaking mamas seem to be here," she acknowledged. "Something tells me I'll be torn to shreds when they discover I'm about to filch one of the eligibles from under their noses."

He laughed, making no attempt to deny it. "Do you like the rooms?"

"They're lovely, thank you," she said, debating whether to deplore his high-handedness in having arranged the move without first consulting her.

"You may have noticed there is only one bedroom?"

With heightened color, Mara admitted that she had taken note of it.

"It's because I disapprove of the custom of quartering husband and wife separately," Roy pointed out virtuously. "If a man's going to leave a warm bed for a cold one after lovemaking, he might just as well stick to a mistress. He . . . did you say something?"

"I did not."

"And it's certainly difficult to quarrel in

comfort if you're not sharing the same bed," Roy pursued.

"You're so sure we'll quarrel?"

"Do fish swim?"

"Your conception of marriage," Mara began haughtily, "is—"

"Speaking of marriage, I found a parson, a Mr. Edgar Bottoms—that is, he took orders, though he doesn't have a living. I promised to use my influence with my father to get him one. Bottoms is here as tutor to Major Lord Quincey's two young sons. Anyhow, he's agreed to perform the ceremony on Friday, the twenty-first, at noon."

"Friday the twenty-first!" gasped Mara. "But that's this week."

"So it is."

"This is Monday."

"All day."

"You're talking about four days from now."

"So I am."

"It's too soon."

He pulled her up from the window seat and into his arms. "*Au contraire*, you lying little hypocrite," he said, having kissed her till she had no breath left to protest with. "It's exactly four and a half years late." He kissed her again, a shade less belligerently. "Do you have a suitable gown?" he asked. "We could probably get something made up in a hurry if you don't."

"I haven't got a white," Mara said slowly.

"I couldn't take my clothes when I left Rydale, so I have only what was kept at Treeways. But there's a cream lace. I had it made for an assembly the family went to in Carlisle before Duggie left—the first time—for the army. Would you like to see it?"

"If you please."

She led him into the bedroom where a smiling, curtsying Belgian maid with round rosy cheeks was still stowing her clothing in cupboards and drawers.

"My batman, Wheeler, will bring my gear over before Friday," Roy said as she pulled aside the gowns in her wardrobe, looking for the cream lace.

"Here it is."

Roy looked with favor at the simple but elegant gown with its overskirt of silver gauze and ruffled chiffon edging around the hem.

"It's a little low-cut for a bride, I expect," Mara said almost apologetically, "but I could use my lace mantilla as a veil and sort of drape it around the neck and shoulders till the ceremony is over."

"That sounds properly modest and virginal," Roy approved gravely.

He began to choke with laughter when Mara blushed poppy-red and cast an agonized look toward the maid.

"Sorry, dear girl, that wasn't meant to embarrass *or* to taunt you. And don't worry about Elise; I doubt she knows more than ten words of English. I was simply overwhelmed at hearing Miss Mara Rydale of Treeways expressing concern for the proprieties. Can it be that you are going to make me a very proper kind of wife, after all?"

"That would depend on which room we are in," Mara answered rashly. Then, as Roy looked toward the big canopied bed, his eyes gleaming wickedly, her face again became one vivid blush.

"Always concentrate on this room, Mara *mia*," he said huskily, with another glance toward the bed so there would be no mistaking his meaning. Then, disregarding the presence of Elise and the universality of the language he was proposing to use, he took Mara into his arms again, allowing his kisses to speak for him.

Other than her hostess, the Comtesse de Lannier, the bride was the only woman present at her wedding four days later. As she descended the wide curved stairway of the de Lannier house to the marble-floored hallway, she was struck by the youthfulness of the six uniformed men who waited for her, from the twenty-two-year-old Prince of Orange to her own twenty-three-year-old bridegroom. But Roy had always seemed so much older than his years!

Duggie gave her his arm, smiling encouragement when he felt the slight trembling of her own. He escorted her quickly into the parlor where the cleric, Mr. Bottoms, was waiting.

Roy saw her answering smile to Duggie and experienced a familiar pang of jealousy. Then he laughed softly to himself as Duggie brought Mara to him and stepped back.

She belonged to *him* now. She was taking *him* as her husband, not slyly, secretly, as though it were something to be ashamed of, but openly, obviously, so that all Brussels would be ringing with the news by nightfall. In a very few minutes she would no longer be his clandestine wife but his wife to claim before all the world. He leaned forward confidently and took her unresisting hand.

Mara stared straight ahead at Mr. Bottoms, hardly seeing the sober cleric but altogether conscious of the insistent pressure of the fingers holding hers. In a very few minutes she would be Lady Roy Irwine, not just on a piece of paper locked away in a jewelry box, but before all the world, properly and proudly and publicly claimed by her husband.

She heard Roy say "I do" in a clear, ringing voice and forced herself to pay attention.

"In deference to the request of Lord Raleigh," said Mr. Bottoms with a sniff meant to convey his disdain for so frivolous a request, "I have omitted the word 'obey' from the marriage service. Mara, do you take Lord Raleigh to be your wedded husband, to have

244

and to hold from this day forth, to love, to honor, and to ob—that is, to love and to honor," he corrected himself hastily, "so long as you both shall live?"

"He only did that for me," Mara explained earnestly to the embarrassed cleric, "so I wouldn't have to worry about breaking a promise." Since he only frowned disapprovingly, she stopped explaining and made her vow.

Roy's shoulders had begun to shake when Mr. Bottoms first expressed his condemnation; by the time Mara said "I do," he was unable to restrain his mirth.

Seeing the uninhibited behavior of the bridegroom, his friends made no further effort to restrain their own laughter.

Into this scene of jollity, the parson tossed a tight-lipped command. "Please place the ring on her finger."

The soldiers all stopped laughing, and Roy looked to Duggie, who began searching frantically in his pockets. His agonized hiss was clearly audible to everyone. "I think I forgot to bring the damn thing!"

Even as the comtesse began pulling off her own wedding band, Mara reached inside the front of her dress. She pulled out a gold chain from which hung a narrow gold band. Mutely she held out both to Roy.

His eyes glowed at her in a fierce mixture of love and passion that set her shivering. With hands that shook, he accepted the gold chain, unclasped it, and slipped the ring off it and onto her finger. "Where it belongs," he whispered.

"I pronounce you man and wife," said Mr. Bottoms with a speed that suggested a heartfelt gladness to be done with the whole irreverent ceremony.

He accepted more cheerfully an envelope that contained his fee and "a letter to my father, the duke," but declined attending the wedding luncheon, which was held in the comtesse's dining room, although Roy had arranged for outside waiters and catering.

"Just as well," said Mara frankly not too long after the cleric's departure. "I don't think he would have appreciated the entertainment."

Since the entertainment was being supplied by the guests, who, unlike the bride, were making greater inroads on the cases of champagne than on the generous supply of food, it consisted for the most part of a selection of lewd songs learned at Eton—almost everyone except the bride, the hostess, and the Oxford-educated Dutch prince having attended those hallowed halls of learning.

When the soldiers exhausted their repertoire, the three hired musicians were allowed to perform and, starting with the charmingly gay young prince, Mara was danced out of the dining room and around the marble-tiled hallway floor by each and every one of the soldiers, including her brother.

"Be happy, Mara," Duggie told her, dropping a light kiss on the top of the blue-black mane, which for this one occasion was decorously bound on top of her head in a handsome braided coronet.

"I shall be," she promised him, eyes shining.

"You've always wanted him, haven't you?" he asked wisely.

Mara laughed happily. No one knew her the way Duggie did. Not even Roy—yet. "Always," she admitted, then winked up at him. "Since I discovered I wasn't allowed to have *you*."

"When are you going to tell him about— that I really *am* your brother?"

"I haven't given it much thought. Anyhow, you know I promised Da that I would never say a word to anyone."

"I don't think that promise was meant to include your husband. Its purpose was mostly to protect Mam and me, and I'm sure we need have no fear that Roy will blab our little family secret to the world. I think you should tell him."

Mara's brows drew together. "Why so insistent?"

"Intuition."

"Male intuition," Mara scoffed. Then, as he gave her a familiar brotherly pinch in a familiar location, "Oh, all right, I'll think about it. Do you think it should be this minute . . . or even tonight"—she slanted a teasing smile up at him—"when he may have other things on his mind than our family tree?"

"I daresay it can wait until after the honeymoon," Duggie told her gravely, then winked at her in turn as Roy came up to claim her.

The musicians played a spirited waltz for the bride and bridegroom and, instead of clasping one of her hands while they danced, Roy put both arms around her waist, whirling her around and around till she clung to him in breathless, dizzy delight.

He kissed her neck and nibbled on her hair as they danced; he whispered "My lady Mara" into one ear and promises for the night ahead into the other till she was incapable of coherent thought and the involuntary spasms in her knees and thighs tangled her legs helplessly together.

Their dance ended in stumbling confusion, and when Roy turned, one supporting arm still around her, to signal the musicians that they had had enough, he and Mara discovered that all their guests had melted silently away.

Chapter Twenty-four

"IT'S ONLY HALF PAST THREE," SAID MARA AS
they mounted the stairs to their fourth-floor
suite.

"I know," said Roy, his arm very firmly
about her. "Why?"

"It's—early, isn't it?" she asked lamely.

"If you mean early for lovemaking," he
said with devastating frankness, "it's never
too early . . . nor, for that matter, too late."
He grinned down at her as they reached the
fourth-floor landing. "If you think I'm going
to sit around for the next few hours waiting
for a conventionally acceptable hour of the
evening to take you to bed, you were never
more mistaken."

Trembling pleasurably, Mara allowed herself to be led into her—no, it was now *their*
bedroom. Elise was there, placing a huge
bowl of spring flowers on Mara's dressing
table. A vase of red roses stood on the ward-

robe, and Mara's nightgown, white with pale blue ribbons and tissue-thin, lay spread out on the bed.

Roy addressed Elise briefly and smilingly in a tongue that seemed to be a mixture of French and Dutch and a little something else. She smiled and blushed and dimpled, curtsied and withdrew.

"What did you say to her?" Mara demanded suspiciously as Roy locked the outer door as well as the one that led to the dressing room.

"I said the wedding lunch was over and the wedding night was about to begin and that she was excused because *I* would maid you tonight."

"You *didn't!*"

"I did," Roy contradicted her, inspecting the nightgown. "This is very pretty. You must model it for me tomorrow morning."

Mara looked at him uncertainly. "I thought —tonight."

"Don't be foolish. The fashion for tonight is *au naturel.*"

Mara gulped as he came up behind her and matter-of-factly started unbuttoning buttons. "Did I tell you how beautiful you looked in your cream-lace wedding gown?"

"No."

"Well, you did—you do, and if I didn't have other things on my mind, I would admire you in it a bit longer. Did I tell you how pleased—

how very happy I am to have you for my *acknowledged* wife?"

"No."

"Well, I am." He kissed first the back of her neck and then, as the last button was undone and he slipped her gown down, a bare shoulder.

"Nervous?" he whispered softly, plucking the pins out of her braided hair till it tumbled down her back in its usual shining disorder.

"A little," Mara admitted, though she wasn't trembling just from nerves.

"That's all right. I am too."

She pushed away to turn and look at him. "Truly?"

"Truly." He brought her back to him. "Come to the bed," he invited, his voice cracking like a schoolboy's.

Mara walked, unresisting, to the bed, kicked off her satin slippers, and lay down sideways. He stood in front of her, pulling off her stockings and then her petticoat. When she was down to her chemise, he dealt with her sudden access of modesty by turning her over on her stomach and disposing of the rest of her undergarments in somewhat rough and ready fashion.

Having gotten her as fashionably *au naturel* as he had decreed—as well as blushing madly into the coverlet—he lightly touched her left buttock with one finger. "You have a black and blue mark."

"I th-think it's where D-Duggie p-pinched me when we were d-dancing."

"In the future," said Roy—and the light kiss that landed on the bruise in no way diminished her blushes—"the only one pinching you *there* is to be me, *comprends-tu?*"

"*Je comprends, mon mari.*" She gave a violent start as his loving, roving hands covered the entire area of her backside.

Roy turned her over, and instinctively her own hands moved to cover her breasts. He shook his head, and she put her arms back to her sides and lay still, allowing his eyes to eat her up and drink her in as he slowly shucked off his uniform and small clothes. Naked as herself, he tumbled her under the covers before he slid in beside her.

As they lay on their backs, with one of Roy's arms under her and Mara's head on his shoulder, his hands made a startlingly intimate survey of his newly acquired territory, the while he carried on a normal if rather one-sided conversation.

"We surely do have interesting weddings, my sweet. Not at all in the dull tradition of Saint George's, Hanover Square."

"Uh. Ah. Umm." Her knees jerked together, almost crushing his hand between them.

"I thought Bottoms would throw a fit when you began that earnest explanation of why I had suggested the change in the service."

"Why . . . ooohh . . . did you?"

"I didn't want to force you to make a promise I knew you could never keep. Tell me about the ring."

"Oh. Ooohh. R-r-r-ring?"

Roy's hands stilled a moment. "Yes, the ring now on your finger that you were wearing around your neck. Has it been there ever since Gretna?"

"I . . . no . . . not after the annulment. I kept it . . . in Mr. Corley's jewelry box—but when I came to Belgium, I c-couldn't b-bear to leave it b-behind."

Even now, his wife again . . . even here, in bed with him, she couldn't confess the shameful weakness that had made her hope and pray with all her heart when she left England with the ring that she would have the right to wear it on her hand again.

Roy smiled to himself, more than pleased with the artless explanation she had given. He turned her on her side and, holding her more firmly, resumed his stroking.

Mara writhed against him as the hands climbed higher and higher between her legs. "Don't, don't, oh please, don't."

"Don't stop? Or don't go on?" asked Roy, a hint of laughter in his voice. She had cried out both before and after he stopped.

"I don't know," quavered Mara, who knew perfectly well. "Wh-what are you doing to me?"

"Trying to prolong your pleasure. And I will even if it kills me."

"It . . . it's killing me."

Roy knelt above her. "Do you mean what I think you mean?"

Silence.

Roy shook her gently. "Say it."

Silence.

"All right, my lady. Two can play your game." He started indulging in such an orgy of touching and tasting that Mara, having tried and failed to wrestle away from him, was reduced to jellied acquiescence.

When he bade her again, "Say it!" she no longer had the slightest desire to fight him.

"I want you now, too," she whispered ardently; then added lest he get the wrongheaded notion that he might have things all his own way, "My lord Raleigh."

Roy pinched her right buttock vigorously. "Now," he said with satisfaction, "you'll have twin bruises."

"You beast!"

"Hush!" He knelt astride her. "Use your lips to better purpose."

She parted them to rail at him but after a while relaxed, then sighed, and finally gave herself completely to the mouth that claimed hers. There would never be anything quite like that night on the mountain, she told herself, but he seemed to know so much more now . . . so many different ways to arouse as well as to satisfy. He was no longer an uncertain, self-doubting schoolboy but very much a man, totally in command, eager, knowledgeable, sharing.

Hours and hours later, when they awoke from the sated sleep that had followed their exhaustive lovemaking, both admitted sheepishly to being ravenous. Roy tucked a nightshirt into a pair of breeches and padded downstairs to see if any servant was available to make up a tray of wedding leftovers.

He came back, carrying the heavy tray himself, to find Mara sitting against the pillows, wearing the tissue-thin nightgown with the pale blue ribbons.

He set the tray on her dressing table and came to sit on the edge of the bed and smile down at her.

"Do you know how often I dreamt of seeing you this way . . . in bed with that hair . . . that wonderful hair of yours"—he rubbed his face in it for a minute—"spread out over a pillow?"

She stared at him, sober and unsmiling.

"What are you thinking about?" he asked huskily.

"This," said Mara, and just as at their meeting in Grammont, her arm flashed out and she dealt him a single cracking slap across the face.

Unprepared, he was knocked both off balance and off the bed. After a moment of stunned surprise, he picked himself up off the floor and went after her. Mara was trying to scramble out of bed on the other side. He got hold of the hair he'd been kissing a minute before and hauled her back to him.

"Now," he said, holding her stomach-down, his knee in the small of her back and one hand still gripping strands of hair, "what the devil was that all about?"

"You know perfectly well."

He released his knee and yanked her upright. "Tell me!" A shake punctuated what was very much an order as he added sardonically, "Do you have some complaint about my lovemaking, perhaps?"

He was startled when Mara wiped away angry tears and blazed right back at him, "Yes, I do. It was too damned good."

"Wha-at?"

"I admit I was just as—carried away—tonight as you, but since—I've had time to think. Did you figure you could fool me? You were as v-v-virgin as me up th-there on the m-m-mountain. Did you think I wouldn't realize you'd been *practicing* a lot since then with other women?"

With a mighty effort of will, he refrained from laughing. She was so very serious, so damn solemn, so quiveringly hurt, it would have been a bad mistake.

He sat down on the bed again, pulling the rigid, resistant figure onto his lap. "I never thought to fool you for a minute, Mara," he assured her gravely.

She turned a little to look at him. "You intended to tell me?"

He considered a minute. "No, I don't think so," he admitted honestly, "not if you didn't ask."

"Then—"

"No." He put two fingers lightly across her lips. "It's been four and a half years, Mara. When I first left you, I didn't want anyone else—only you. But then when I went to the Peninsula . . . well, you had opened up a world of new delight to me, and I found after a while that I wanted that world badly. I needed it even if I couldn't have you. I even thought—well, I won't pretend my purpose was noble, but I did think I might be a hell of a lot more use to you someday if I had more of what you call practice."

"Suppose I had done the same? Suppose before the wedding I told you that I'd been practicing for your sake? Or just because I liked being made love to?"

"I'd have probably beaten you black and blue out of sheer jealousy, but I would have married you just the same."

"*You'd* have beaten me black and blue, but *I'm* not supposed to give you a single slap."

"You certainly are," he soothed, "now that I know the reason. Here. I'll turn the other cheek." He did so. "Slap it as hard as you want, darling. More than once, if it will make you feel better."

"It won't," sniffed Mara dolefully. "Why didn't you write more? Why didn't you send for me? Why—"

"I couldn't do any of those things you wanted of me or I wanted of you. Not from behind enemy lines."

It took a minute to sink in. Then Mara wriggled off his knees and knelt between them so she could look up at him. "*Behind* enemy lines. You—"

"Look, my sweet, admittedly Wellington prefers young sprigs of nobility about him, but even so . . . why would you think he'd welcome with open arms another nineteen-year-old with no military experience? It was my proficiency at languages they needed on the Peninsula, an Englishman who could be French or Spanish at will."

"A spy. Oh dear God, it's *dangerous* to be a spy!"

"Not so dangerous as fighting," he assured her gayly. "In one of the only two engagements I was ever in—Saint Pierre—I got wounded. If I hadn't, I might have been able to come home to you last year."

"I'm glad now I didn't know," she said fervently. "I would rather have been furious at you—the way I was—instead of frightened for all those years. It *was* for all those years?"

"Most of them," he admitted. "Mara, you do understand," he reminded her a bit sternly, "this is not to go beyond this room?"

"Not even Duggie."

"Duggie knows," he said curtly. "He was my courier several times."

She rose stiffly from her crouched position. "The both of you! Oh, God!"

Roy stood up, too, and said quietly, "Let's eat. I brought all sorts of good things from our wedding luncheon for our wedding supper and a bottle of champagne as well."

"I've lost my appetite."

"You'll get it back when you sit down to the table. We'll take the tray to our sitting room."

As she started to turn away, he pulled her back to face him. "Is this the same girl who talked about following the drum all her life?" he asked teasingly. Then his voice changed. "Mara, if you can't take being a soldier's wife, you should not have married a soldier."

He had been sure she would respond to a challenge and was not surprised when her head jerked up and she tossed the mane of hair back over her shoulders. Even as her eyes glistened with unshed tears, she grabbed the bottle of champagne from the tray, shaking it thoroughly as she danced ahead of him to the sitting room.

When he uncorked the champagne, standing close to her, it spouted up like a fountain, pouring down over her head and face and the tissue-thin bodice of her nightgown.

He lapped the champagne from her hair on top and licked it off her cheeks and neck, then her sopping tissue-clad breasts.

"Mara . . . Mara . . . Mara?"

As he drank, he had pulled her down to the carpet, which was faded and old but satisfyingly soft.

"You mean—dessert before dinner?"

"That's just what I mean."

"All right . . . but finish the champagne first, please, it's trickling down my stomach."

While she wriggled out of the clinging wet gown, Roy lay on his back, singing softly.

> *"But might I of Jove's nectar sip*
> *Then I'd not ask for wine. . . ."*

Then he started sipping champagne.

Chapter Twenty-five

THEY HAD THREE DAYS UNINTERRUPTED BY military duties before Roy was sent overnight to Ghent. On his return, when it became apparent that his days as well as some of his nights belonged to the army, not to her, Mara returned to her schoolteaching and her nursing, with Roy's batman, Wheeler, her constant escort.

The social life in Brussels was gay and active, and invitations to the new-wedded couple abounded, but they accepted none that Roy didn't label with a groan, "Compulsory." Their rare few hours together were far too precious to share.

On the first of May, ten days after their wedding, she was at her school in Grammont when Roy stopped by unexpectedly. Her first glad smile faded when she saw his taut expression.

Leaving the nursery group she was tending with their coloring books, Mara walked outside with her husband.

"I won't be home tonight when you get there, my sweet. I'm not sure when I'll be back."

"Where are you going?"

He shook his head. "I'm sorry, darling. No questions. If anyone asks, I'm away for the day . . . Ostend . . . Ghent . . . and try if you can to seem carefree and untroubled."

"Have I reason to be otherwise?"

"I always come back."

"I seem to remember your saying that after our *first* wedding. You didn't."

"Word of honor, the end of the month at the latest."

"I swear I'll make you regret it if you break that promise."

He caught and held her, kissed her eyes and her hair and her softly yielding mouth, then set her away from him. "Wheeler will look after you. He knows what to do in any emergency. Duggie, too . . . I saw him at headquarters this morning. Stay out of trouble, please."

"I'm the one supposed to say that," Mara told him, lips trembling.

"Not really." He walked her toward the post where his horse was tied, loosed the reins, and mounted.

He smiled down at her as two mothers walked through the gate and looked over at them curiously. "I love you, my lady Mara," he said, then was gone without a backward look, setting his horse at a gallop and taking the low fence.

Mara closed her eyes, hearing those wonderful words over and over. *I love you, my lady Mara.* When he returned she would be able to tell him how long and how much she had loved him, too.

She turned and trudged back into the schoolhouse. She was determined to behave like a "soldier's wife"; she must be deserving of his love.

The month of May went by and Roy did not come back. Mara showed a serene and smiling face to all during the day. Only at night, when she was alone, did she give way to her terrors.

"You look awful," Duggie told her with brotherly frankness one night when he had dragged her out to a dinner at the Hotel de Ville, to be followed by a concert at the Guinguette Tivoli. He had told her in no uncertain terms when she refused that she was damned well going to come when he had gone to so much trouble to get the coveted seats . . . to say nothing of the scandalous price of the tickets.

"You should have left me at home," Mara said just as ungraciously.

"I know I should have, but since I didn't, for God's sakes, try to look as though you're enjoying yourself, not as though your dearest friend just died."

There was a moment's stricken silence; then he took her hand. "Mara, I didn't mean—"

Mara began to giggle. "Oh, come on, Duggie, I know it was just a manner of speaking. You're the one with the ghastly face now. You know, this fish isn't bad, but I'd like to try a little of your veal . . . it looks delicious. Tell me about the concert," she chattered on. "Who will be singing tonight?"

When June came, she no longer returned to Brussels in the evenings but stayed on in Grammont, where there was enough to do to keep her busy day and night. She wanted to be busy. She needed to be! It was better to be busy than to have hours alone to think.

Wheeler objected to her plans, telling her mournfully that "the captain" would censure *him*. Mara only smiled her impudent gamine's smile. "No, he won't, Wheeler," she assured him cheerily. "He'll place the blame squarely where it belongs"—she tapped her shoulders—"on these."

Stubborn as herself, the batman insisted on sleeping in the same house where she slept, which presented no difficulties the first week when she was helping the wife of Major Munson to nurse her three little girls who all had the measles; he was satisfied with a cot in the kitchen.

The second week she stayed with Captain Lord Everleigh's eighteen-year-old bride who was momentarily expecting her first child and was terrified. Mara shared Mrs. Everleigh's small room in a two-bedroom Belgian farmhouse; the farmer and his family were crowded into the larger room. Captain Everleigh slept in the barn, and so did the determined Corporal Wheeler.

The baby, a boy, was born on the tenth of June, with Mara and the midwife in attendance. On the sixteenth came word that the French had begun their move the previous day and the British regiments in Brussels had been on the march all through the night, many of the officers, including the duke, setting off to war direct from the Duchess of Richmond's ball in white dress pantaloons and embroidered coats.

Captain Everleigh, who had already arranged for his wife's transport to Antwerp, properly escorted, speeded her on her way. Mara, urged by all to go with her, obstinately declined.

Wheeler all but wrung his hands in dismay. "The captain said as how, if war broke out before he got back, I was to tie you on the back of a horse, if I had to, and see you safe to Antwerp."

"Wheeler, there is no way in hell you could get me to Antwerp . . . or, if you succeeded, make me stay there. My brother is here, and I . . . I intend to wait for my husband. No more arguments, please; I'm going with the army. If you're coming with me, get the horses."

The horses were gone, and Mara's donkey cart, too, possibly stolen by some British in the mad stampede to seek refuge in Antwerp, possibly by Belgians to sell at enormous profit to those seeking means of escape.

Mara shrugged when she was given this bad news. "Then we walk."

She started stuffing a knapsack with a few extra pairs of stockings, a flannel nightgown, and whatever supplies the farmer's wife could spare, three ham pies, cold chicken, and a cheese. At the last minute she added a bottle of her wedding champagne, hopefully brought from Brussels for her reunion with Roy.

Wheeler went to draw his army rations and returned with a three-day supply to say he had met an old soldier friend, William Leakey, who had told him the regiment was marching out of Grammont. It would probably be safer—unless she had sensibly changed her mind—for them to march in its tail.

Mara put one of Captain Everleigh's jackets on under her hooded cloak for added protection from the rain, grabbed up her knapsack with its precious contents, including the purse with all her Belgian money. At the last moment she asked for and received the oilcloth covering from the kitchen table, offering a coin in payment to the farmer's wife.

It was a miserable day, and they marched on and on through what seemed like an endless field of mud. Mara's knapsack seemed to get so much heavier, she soon decided that wine inside the stomach would be better than a bottle weighting her down. She and Wheeler stopped to lunch on army rations, ham pie, and champagne. Three soldiers who lingered, watching them drink, were invited to share the bottle. The five passed it around till the last drop was done.

"Bless you, my pretty miss," said one of the soldiers, hurling the empty bottle over a hedge. Mara merely smiled to herself—it had been apparent from their free and casual manner that they thought her a lady of easy virtue following the army—but the impudent farewell was too much for Wheeler, who had thoroughly disapproved of the entire democratic exchange.

"If you come across Captain Irwine, a staff officer, or Lieutenant MacTavish of the Fifty-second," he said haughtily, "pray tell them where and when you saw Lady Irwine, under the charge of Corporal Wheeler."

The soldiers looked abashed only till they saw Mara's broad smile and wink.

"Please do look out for them." She repeated the names. "Captain Irwine, my husband. Lieutenant MacTavish, my brother. Good-bye, men. Good luck to you."

"Good luck to you, my lady." They continued to wave till they were out of sight.

The miserably wet and ragtail regiment disported itself all over a big farm that night, officers in the house, men all over the barns. Mara was so lucky as to get a toolshed all to herself, with Wheeler stubbornly guarding it from outside, despite her plea that he come in from the rain with her or else sleep in a barn with the soldiers.

A voice outside the shed suddenly shouted, "Mara! Mara!" and she flung the door open to be enveloped in Duggie's arms.

"I ought to wring your neck. Roy said he arranged for you to be taken to Antwerp."

"I wouldn't go. How could I—not knowing whether you and he were safe?"

"Well, he was not only safe but in a towering rage this morning when he heard you were with the army."

"This morning! Oh, Duggie, Duggie, he's safe, he's well, you saw him?"

"I not only saw, I heard him. They probably heard him all the way to France demanding why I hadn't tied you hand and foot."

"As though you could have!"

"That's what I told him . . . not that I even got the chance to try. We were called into action so fast yesterday, there wasn't any possibility of my getting to Grammont."

"Tell me about Roy. Where is he now? Why was he so many weeks coming back?"

"He's with the rest of the staff, probably. I'm not sure where, except that I'd take a wager he's undoubtedly warm, well fed, and comfortable at the moment, which is more than I can say for you or myself. As for where he was—first in France, then with the French army. He said he had the devil's own time getting back to our lines and then, when he finally managed to, he was nearly shot for his pains by a couple of our overzealous Life Guardsmen."

Mara said in a choked voice, "I had almost given up hope I would ever see him again."

"How could you be so daft? The lad's got nine lives, and he's not even used up half."

Mara couldn't help laughing, he sounded so much like Angus.

"How did you know where to find me?" she asked, and Duggie grinned.

"From some soldiers you shared your champagne with. That made quite an impression. That and your being a ladyship. Come on, I've got an extra horse—don't ask from where. He's a pretty sorry nag, but he should last long enough to get you and Wheeler to Brussels. I'd take you myself, but I have to be back with my regiment."

"Duggie . . . no!"

"Mara, yes." Seeing the mulish set to her mouth, he changed his tone. "Think, lass," he cajoled, "you'll only be a hindrance to us here—Wheeler as well as Roy and me. The army needs him more than you do, and we all need our minds free to do our jobs. Brussels is where Roy thinks you are—it's where he'll come looking for you if he gets the

chance. Out here"—he waved both hands—
"it would be a miracle if he found you. It was
only by the greatest good chance that I did."

No other argument could have convinced
Mara as much as the thought of Roy in
Brussels, looking for her, while she wan-
dered through the godforsaken muddy fields
of rye looking for him.

"I'll go," she said meekly. "Here." She
emptied the food that was left into a big
scarf, tied it at the ends, threw the oilcloth
over his wet shoulders. Duggie accepted this
bounty gratefully and helped her onto the
"sorry nag" behind Wheeler.

"Take care," he told her brusquely.

"*You* take care, Duggie."

"I think—excuse the liberty—it would be
best if you held me about the waist, my lady,"
said Wheeler primly.

Laughing softly at the formality after what
they'd been through together, Mara put her
arms around his waist, and they traveled
through the night to Brussels.

Chapter Twenty-six

THE NEXT MORNING THE WOUNDED BEGAN pouring into Brussels, the lucky ones staggering, straggling, and limping on their own two legs rather than sharing the lot of their less fortunate comrades, condemned to be crammed six together into the abominably uncomfortable tilt wagons which jolted them mercilessly all the long hard journey.

In the morning Mara went with her medical kit into the streets, moving among the injured to render what aid she could. By afternoon's end, with the help of the comtesse and her few remaining servants, the de Lannier house had been turned into an improvised hospital.

All the beds had been brought down from the upper stories and the empty ballroom converted into a huge ward. Two small antechambers served as private rooms for those more seriously wounded. Elise and the cook brewed possets and kept a huge iron pot of soup stocked with vegetables and several poor scrawny chickens constantly on the boil to feed the soldiers.

The footmen fetched and carried, turned patients, or held them down while Mara or the surgeon who came periodically stitched or bandaged. They all assisted at amputations.

Mara asked for news of Captain Irwine or Lieutenant MacTavish of any new arrival who was conscious. As long as daylight lasted, she went out in the streets in search of more wounded and more news. Toward late afternoon, searching among the stretcher cases, two to a wagon, she came upon Duggie, his face so blackened by gunpowder and his uniform in such tatters, she might not have recognized him if he had not called out to her in a weak dazed voice.

"Mara, is it . . . you . . . love . . . thought still . . . on the field . . . noise still in my ears." He shook his head fretfully.

"It's me, Duggie darling, it's me." She kissed his feverish forehead, then his cracked, dry lips. "We'll have you comfortable in just a little while."

She directed the driver the few blocks to the de Lannier house. Three men were enlisted to carry Duggie inside to a small room at the back of the house. The men cut off his boots while Mara unwrapped the bloodied wrapping around his knee and carefully sponged off the gaping wound that had shattered the bone and extended along his thigh.

"We must have the surgeon at once," she told the comtesse over her shoulder, amazed at the steadiness of her own voice as she wiped his face clean and dribbled wine between his lips.

The surgeon had not been found by the time Duggie was clean and comfortable and wearing one of Roy's fine white lawn nightshirts brought down by Elise from the stripped bedroom of the fourth-floor honeymoon suite.

Mara sat beside his bed, holding one limp hand and damping his face with a cool cloth.

Presently he opened his eyes.

"Mara?"

"Yes, love?"

"The leg—it . . . must . . . come off?"

"Yes, love. I fear so."

There was a long silence during which she brought the hand to her lips and her tears fell upon it.

"No more . . . I'll go . . . for a soldier," said Duggie after a while.

"There's always Treeways," said Mara. "When I get my money from Griselda, I'll buy out Mr. Benton's share for you."

He smiled weakly, only half listening, and closed his eyes. Mara looked anxiously toward the door, then got up and peered outside. Where was that damned sawbones?

"Mara."

She hurried to the bed again. "Yes, Duggie."

"Remember . . . when you were little . . . and had a nightmare?"

"I—I remember."

She used to run from her solitary bed to the bigger one in the bigger room Duggie shared with Donnie. The two would let her crawl in between them. Snuggled against Duggie, she had felt safe and secure; nothing could go wrong with her world when he was there, holding on to her.

"I—m-my turn. I'm f-frightened, Mara."

She kicked off her shoes and tore the buttons off her dress in her eagerness to be rid of it. Leaving both in a heap on the floor, she crawled into bed beside Duggie, on the side away from his wound. Her bare arms encircled him in a fiercely protective embrace; his head turned like a baby's seeking her bosom.

"Ah, that's good, that's so good," she barely heard him murmur.

He drifted off to sleep, and she half sat, half lay, afraid to stir, afraid to disturb him.

Roy found them together, the shoes and dress lying on the floor, seemingly a result of the same abandoned passion she had often shown removing them for him. Her bare arms were around Duggie; his face lay against her chemise-covered breasts.

Mara was speechless for a moment, so overwhelmed to see him whole and well that she utterly misread the pain and fury on his face.

Only when she heard his hoarse whisper, "You goddamned whore!" did she understand and lay Duggie down, with one quick glance first to make sure he had not wakened.

Roy saw that glance and was doubly stricken. Even now—always!—her first thought was for Duggie.

He had traveled this bloody night, an hour and a half, reeling with exhaustion, and would have to travel the same time back, all for the sake of twenty minutes to hold her in his arms, knowing she was his . . . only twenty minutes, and instead this.

As Mara slipped out of the bed and faced him, head held high, Roy's rage mounted. She had the effrontery to face him with no shame for her chemise and petticoat and being found bedded with his good friend Duggie MacTavish! God damn her to hell! His hand came up and the force of his slap slammed her face into her shoulder.

"When this is over," he told her, "I'm sending you home to my family in England to be properly schooled for your station in life . . . something I seem unable to have taught you."

She smiled crookedly for all of her flaming cheek and aching jaw. "And if I don't choose to go?"

"Then you may choose the scandal of divorce, by God, which won't do *his* career any good."

He flung himself out of the room, and Mara slowly, tremblingly, after another glance to make sure that Duggie still slept, slipped on her shoes again and buttoned herself into her dress.

The Belgian surgeon who arrived presently was as skilled as the good Dr. Hume, the comtesse assured her, and Mara could not argue with his decision that the leg must come off from the middle of the thigh. Indeed, he expressed surprise that it had not been done on the field, where lacerated knees, ankles, and elbows were traditionally lopped right off.

After the patient had been rendered almost painlessly drunk, the surgery took place in the area set aside in the kitchen. Then Duggie was taken back to the small bedchamber, singing one of the ribald songs that had been the entertainment at her wedding. He lay quiet for a while and then began to toss around so in his fever, he had to be tied down.

All through the night, Mara knelt, damping his brow and body, murmuring consolation and endearments. Just before dawn, the fevered eyes seemed to clear, and he asked intelligibly, intelligently, "Is Roy safe?"

"Safe and well," Mara forced herself to say gaily. "Not so much as a scratch."

"Good old Roy." He gave a small, tired sigh. "He'll take care of you, my lass."

"Of course he will." Tears glistened on the edges of her lashes. By the time they had rolled down her cheeks, her dearly loved brother was dead.

The bells rang out the news of victory at Waterloo while Duggie was being buried in the Protestant cemetery. The same wagon that had carried his body to the gravesite took Mara and her small packed trunk to Antwerp right afterward.

The comtesse had begged and implored her to wait on in Brussels for her husband, but Mara, still in shock from Duggie's death and what she considered Roy's betrayal, had only smiled a frozen smile and shaken her head. "Give him this, please, madame."

The envelope she held out contained two wedding rings . . . the narrow gold band from Gretna and the wider circle of diamond baguettes that Duggie had forgotten to bring to her second wedding in Brussels. She had worn them both these last eight weeks.

The slip of paper she had enclosed with the two rings contained neither a greeting nor a signature, only the brief cold comment: *I choose the scandal of divorce.*

The first familiar face Mara saw in Antwerp as she tried to secure passage for England was Mr. Bottoms, who had performed her marriage ceremony. He was returning to England, he explained, to present his letter of introduction from Lord Raleigh to his noble father.

"I thought you had employment with Major Lord Quincey," exclaimed Mara, dismayed at the prospect of his company all during their passage.

"Lord Quincey was suddenly ordered on a diplomatic mission to America . . . is leaving, in fact, this very day. I had no desire to go to that savage country, especially since . . ." He coughed, slightly embarrassed. "My letter to the duke, you know . . . I prefer to seek out a living in England."

"Yes, of course, of course," said Mara, suddenly struck by a brilliant notion. "But the Quinceys—"

"One is sorry to disappoint them, but *America* was never indicated when I took the position."

"I know of someone who might be interested in the post," she told him eagerly. "Have the Quinceys left yet?"

"They go by canal boat to Ostend in the next hour and from there across the ocean. I fear it is too late for your friend."

With as much patience as she could muster, Mara listened to his detailed directions and, followed by her grumbling wagoneer, hurried in search of the canal boat.

She was sure that she was in time when she saw the group standing on the dock, the tearful young matron holding a young boy by either hand, a frankly weeping nursemaid carrying a small girl, and the harassed-looking major in shako and cloak overseeing all.

Mara came hurrying up to the group.

"Lord Quincey? Lady Quincey?" she addressed them breathlessly.

"Yes, ma'am?"

"I was recommended by Mr. Bottoms, who—"

Lady Quincey stiffened. Lord Quincey exclaimed, "That prosy coward!"

Both were disarmed by Mara's giggle. "Isn't he, though, but he did happen to mention you need a tutor who isn't averse to going to America, and I'm not, so—" She looked up at them hopefully.

"A tutor, my dear Miss . . .?"

"Rydale," said Mara unhesitatingly.

"Miss Rydale, what I require is not a governess but a tutor to prepare my sons for Harrow."

"That's me," she assured them happily. "I can ground them thoroughly in Latin, Greek, French, mathematics, history, and literature."

As they stared at her disbelievingly she began to rattle out some passages from Pliny, then switched to Plato, and finally conducted a running commentary in French on the quality and materials of Lady Quincey's gown and bonnet. She finished triumphantly in English, "I would expect one hundred and fifty pounds per annum paid quarterly and my passage home anytime after one year."

"You're hired," said Lord Quincey.

"Reginald"—his wife tugged at his arm—"don't you think . . . ?"

"Good Lord, Madelaine, she's a gift from God, take her."

"Well, I suppose so," she began weakly, even as her husband said to Mara, "How much time do you need? Where are your things?"

"In that trunk." She pointed to the wagon. "I only need time to write and post a letter home."

"I'll see that it goes in the diplomatic pouch from Ostend. You there, bring that trunk."

Perched on her trunk aboard the canal ship, with a notebook on her lap, Mara stared out to sea with tear-dimmed eyes, then resolutely began her letter.

My Beloved Family,

No doubt you have already learned from the casualty lists. If not, then it is with breaking heart that I must tell you how our Duggie died in my arms . . .

Chapter Twenty-seven

MORE THAN TWO YEARS PASSED AFTER WAterloo before Mara saw England again. She was with the Quinceys all that time, a satisfactory situation for all.

The Quincey boys were a devilish pair, who kept her far too busy to have much time left over for brooding during her first terrible year when the loss of Duggie was an unhealed wound within her and the bitterness of Roy's lack of faith like a canker eating at her flesh.

During her second year time had healed her hurts a little. She began to be known and go about more. Washington City, burned by the British in the late foolish war which had taken men and troops away from Wellington at Waterloo, was a robust and fascinating if not very elegant town. The lovely Miss Rydale was no lowly governess there, as she would have been in London, but as appealing to Americans as any ladyship.

If not for Treeways—if there had been no Emma and Angus and Donnie—Mara could have settled for life in a country where a governess was no less valued a person than a lord's lady. As it was she wrote to Cumbria that she missed them all and the hills of home as well. She would return one day soon. After all, she was past two and twenty. Her father no longer had control over her destiny; she had no husband, thank God, to order her life.

Then in late autumn of 1817 she received a letter from her attorney, written to hasten her homecoming. "Your father's physician is of the opinion that Sir Cuthbert will not last out the year," Mr. Firkin wrote in his precise way, "and he is most anxious to see you one last time. You need have no anxiety that he will importune you about marriage; he has long since made a generous settlement on your cousin Gray-Gordon for his disappointment, and his will is most properly changed back, leaving Rydale Park and all else to you."

Within days of receiving this letter Mara was on her way home, arriving in Cumberland, as her own father had done a quarter-century before, in sufficient time to attend the paternal deathbed.

After the funeral Mara made short shrift of

the visiting relatives and herself went to stay for a while at Treeways.

"It's such a lonely, ghost-ridden house, Rydale is," she told them all, shivering. "I can't face living alone there just yet."

"Sir Cuthbert was right in one respect," murmured Emma a bit sadly. "It's a huge house in need of children."

"Well, it's going to have them," said Mara. "I've decided for the next several years at least to turn it into a home for unwed girls . . . to live there while they're waiting to have their babies and for a little time afterward till they're trained for some work and can get themselves established. What do you think?"

"Lord a mercy!" exclaimed Nurse in shock. "Your father would spin over in his grave at the very notion."

"Then the Rydale mausoleum is going to be rather active," said Mara irreverently, "because I intend to discuss with Mr. Firkin this very day the monies I will need. It's a rather costly project. Also"—she turned toward Angus, suddenly serious—"I spoke to Mr. Benton last night and learned that he is extremely eager to retire and move to his sister's home in Bath. I agreed to buy his share of the farm, though I left the terms to be decided upon by the two of you. I'll fix up the Great House for myself . . . otherwise, it will all eventually go to Donnie."

"Good God, Mara, I don't know what to say," muttered Donnie, dazed.

"Say *nothing*, brother," Mara counseled him firmly. "I find I am more my father's daughter than ever I dreamed. I will not rest contented until I see Treeways—cottage and Great House both—all populated with little MacTavishes."

In the midst of the general laughter she escaped all expressions of gratitude by going to her room to change into her old blue riding dress. Then she mounted Arrow for the trip to Carlisle.

She was happy and smiling when she walked into Mr. Firkin's office; she had every expectation of leaving it the same way. No doubt he would hem and haw and express grave doubts about the expenditure of so much money, not to the benefit of the estate, but in the end he would have no choice but to carry out her wishes. Briefly, concisely, she outlined her plans.

Mr. Firkin looked more disturbed than she had anticipated. "Oh, dear me, dear me, this is most disturbing, such expensive schemes, and the farm for the MacTavishes too. Dear Miss Mara, I am afraid, *very* afraid, it is out of my power to aid you."

"You told me just days ago that I was an extremely wealthy woman."

"You are, indeed, you are, but it would be impossible for me to disburse any such sums as you are suggesting without the consent of

your legal—that is, to say, the legal custodi-
an of your money."

"There is none!" shouted Mara, jumping
up. "My father is dead, and I am past two
and twenty."

"But you are forgetting . . . oh, dear me, I
knew this would cause trouble when you
married without proper settlements being
made." He shook his head disapprovingly.
"A course I would never advocate when a
woman has property. Hence, by law, your
husband owns and controls everything that
you inherited . . . money, lands, even, I regret to say, the very clothes on your back."

"But — I — don't — have — a — husband,"
Mara enunciated as though talking to an
idiot. "He divorced me."

"If he did, my dear Lady Irwine," said Mr.
Firkin, taking the bull by the horns with this
bold use of the despised, discarded name, "I
can only say that he seems not to be aware of
it. I had a letter from him, written after he
learned from Mrs. MacTavish of your father's death and your return. He said he
wished you to have—his own words 'a generous allowance,' and that there was no need
for me to apply to him regarding 'any reasonable expenditure' contemplated by you.

"I fear, though," he added, glancing bravely into the face of flaming fury bent to his as
she flattened her palms on his desk, looking
as though she might leap over it any minute
the better to challenge him. "I fear, though,"

he repeated, "that the costs of purchasing a farm for the MacTavishes and renovating Rydale Park so as to fit it for a housing facility for unmarried mothers and unclaimed children can in no wise be deemed 'reasonable expenditures.' For these I *would* require Lord Raleigh's permission."

"Lord Raleigh's permission!" Mara's soaring voice caused the three clerks in the outer office simultaneously to stop writing in their ledgers. "I'll see him in hell before I require *his* permission for what *I* do."

Noting Mr. Firkin's beleaguered look, she suddenly flopped back in her chair. "Forgive me." She smiled disarmingly across at him. "I haven't been so angry in years. Even from this distance, he can still . . . ah, well, the first order of business appears to be to find out whether I am or am not married. Then we can proceed from there."

She rose briskly again. "Do you happen to know where Lord Raleigh is living?"

He looked down at the folder on his desk. "Irwine House on—"

"Albemarle Street, London. I know."

It was a familiar direction from the period of letter-writing before he went into the army and gave a touch of déjà vu to the sensations she experienced mounting the steps of the Georgian brick house some ten days later. She sent her maid, Annie, to wait in the hackney at the curb while she vigorously sounded the knocker.

"Miss Mara Rydale to see Lord Raleigh Irwine," she informed the imposingly tall butler who bent, one hand to his ear, forcing her to repeat this request.

He showed her into a small writing room and was back barely before Mara had begun to inspect a small hedged-in garden.

"My master regrets, madam, he does not recognize the name."

"He won't see me?" Mara asked incredulously.

"He will not see a *Miss* Rydale . . . perhaps, by your proper name," the butler hinted.

As Mara's hands clasped beneath her chin and she bit down on whitened knuckles, the butler stooped to retrieve the reticule she had dropped. "Please inform Lord Raleigh," she said colorlessly, "that Lady Raleigh begs a few moments of his time."

He was back even more quickly than before. "Please follow me, my lady."

She was ushered into a cheerful breakfast parlor. The handsome gray-haired man at the head of the table rose immediately; Roy, to the right of him, rose stumblingly.

"Mara," he said, and then again, "Mara . . . Father," to the gray-haired man, "this is my wife. Mara, my father, the Duke of Ghent."

"How do you do, your Grace?" said Mara clearly.

"I do very well, my dear. This is a long-awaited pleasure," said the duke, taking her hand. "Pray be seated. Will you join us for breakfast?"

"I am rather hungry," Mara admitted.

"When were you not?" asked Roy as they all sat down together. The familiar smile broke through the gravity of his face, and Mara was a little relieved. He was twenty-five, and until he smiled, he had looked thirty, with weary lines about the eyes and creases across his forehead. She was damned if she was about to feel sorry for *him*.

Mara buttered a bit of muffin. "Do you mind, my lord, if we discuss our private affairs before your father?"

"My father is fully aware what a sorry mess we have made of our private affairs, so, no, Mara, I do not much mind and my name is still Roy."

"Did you or did you not get divorced from me?"

"I did not."

"Why the hell not?"

The carefully listening duke looked startled, then amused.

"I didn't want to."

"Indeed? That isn't *my* recollection."

"Yes," said Roy bitterly, "I always knew you'd have that to fling in my teeth. I said it in a moment of passion, a time of misunderstanding, and when the madness was over, I would have knelt at your feet to beg your forgiveness . . . only you weren't there to be knelt to."

"And neither was Duggie," Mara reminded him bitingly. "Your filthy thoughts wronged him as much . . . more . . . than they ever did me."

"Do you think I don't know—didn't realize then that any hope I had of getting you back died with Duggie? Damn it to hell, Mara"—his voice cracked and the duke silently signaled the servants to leave—"he was my friend, a brother; I loved him too."

"Yes, your brother, your friend whom you loved, yet you thought—"

"Because, where you were concerned, in spite of the friendship and the love, I was always jealous of him. I felt that way until after Waterloo, when Emma told me he was your blood brother . . . maybe even still then. Can't you understand that? Almost from the beginning I strove to get from you what *he* always got without trying . . . to be first in your heart. If he had lived, I might have." A shaking hand shadowed his eyes. "But dying, he won, hands down."

"This is impossible!" said Mara, her throat aching with the pain of tears held back. "I didn't come here to wrangle with you, Roy, just to reach an understanding. I want the use of my own money. Can't we still come to an agreement about a divorce?"

She looked from Roy's carefully expressionless face to his father's. The duke shook his head. "Not without an act of Parliament and a disastrous effect on Roy's political career, my dear," he told her directly, "and I can't believe you mean my son that much harm."

"Of course I don't wish him harm. We were . . . we were . . . But I want to be able to run my own life. I want to buy Treeways for Donnie and I want Rydale as a home for unmarried mothers and their babies—their *bastards*. You do know, don't you," she flung at Roy, "that without Angus MacTavish, Duggie would have been just another Rydale bastard?"

"As I said, Emma told me everything."

The duke cleared his throat. "I have a suggestion." They both looked at him expectantly.

"To carry out *her* plans, Mara needs her money. To carry out *his*, Roy needs the *appearance* of a respectable marriage. If you would winter here in London each year, my dear Mara, to hostess for Roy and for me—which his mother is not well enough to do—then the rest of the year you could spend in Cumberland, seeing to your own interests."

"What would you expect of me?" Mara asked suspiciously.

"As I said, hostessing here at home, attendance at important dinners and small parties—these could be limited this year out of respect to your mourning. Next year, I'm afraid, you would have to be presented at Court."

She made a gesture of distaste but pursued doggedly, "And a *written* agreement about my money?"

"By all means, a written agreement," her father-in-law said suavely.

"And"—she flushed slightly but stared straight at Roy and listed her final condition —"a private apartment of my own?"

"So private," said her husband before his father could speak for him, "that you may be sure I will never step foot in it. Shall we go upstairs now and choose your rooms?"

He rose so abruptly that Mara found herself rising, too, still hungry. There was a cane hooked over the chair next to Roy's. She noticed that he seized and used it, limping a little as he led the way to the staircase.

"You've hurt yourself?" She asked it mostly for something to say in this impossible situation.

"A minor hunting mishap," he said dismissingly. "I think you might like the Blue Suite. It goes with your coloring," he added coolly, "and it's as far away as you can get from my rooms."

Chapter Twenty-eight

THE WINTER WAS A SURPRISINGLY ENJOY-
able one for Mara. For all that she despised
small talk and the inanities of social life, she
had discovered, she told her husband and the
duke quite affably, that she could have just
as good a time at London parties as at the
Zoological Gardens, "for at least during parties, the animals aren't caged and perform of
their own free will."

She had breakfast with the two men most
mornings and dined with them most nights.
During the day they were busy about their
own concerns and Mara was busy with
hers.

A winter in London was no bad thing, she
was discovering. The duke had put her in
touch with aid societies and charitable
groups involved in helping unwed mothers
as well as those who ran orphanages.

"Dear God," she reported back to him,

shuddering, "mostly I am learning what *not* to do when I establish my home."

"You must beware of making illegitimacy appealing," he warned her once.

"As though it *could* be when you consider how these poor girls are treated!" she flared. "Can they not be regarded as human? Cannot the so-called good women look at them and think that there, but for the grace of God, go they?"

"Perhaps," said the duke rather cynically, "but I doubt it. You will find the greatest opponents of what you do, I suspect, among those same self-styled good women."

Roy was helpful, too, frequently adding names to her increasingly long list of women workers who could advise and counsel her.

"Some of these understand the business end," he told her one day, handing over a paper with several names. "You must realize by now, Mara, that this project is going to take more than a fat purse and a warm heart."

"I know," Mara said ruefully. "I'm not nearly so impulsive as you think. I do intend mixing a few knowledgeable business heads in with my motherly matrons to ensure against bankruptcy." She looked over the notes he had scribbled after each name. "Thank you, this will be a great help to me."

As she spoke, she half put out her hand to him, then, remembering suddenly, snatched it back.

Her face went red and his turned white.

"I don't bite," he told her scathingly. "Nor will you catch anything if you touch me."

"I'm sorry," said Mara on a sob, and ran up the stairs to her rooms.

It rained all that day and the next, a dreary February rain, and both days Mara rode around London, keeping appointments and getting thoroughly wet on mad dashes from carriage to doorstep. By the end of the second day, when she arrived home at Irwine House in the late afternoon, she was coughing and sneezing and red-eyed.

Roy limped out into the hallway as the butler took her cloak and bonnet. He looked at his wife's damp face, wet hair, and sopping skirts.

"You little fool!" he said without heat. "Get out of those wet things at once."

Mara raised her eyebrows mockingly. "At once? You mean here and now?"

He grinned. "May I amend that? Go up to your room first."

"Aye, aye, Captain." She ran up the stairs, laughing, with Roy just behind her.

When she opened the door of her room, he called to her maid, "See that Lady Irwine has a hot bath, Annie, and is properly dried. I'll send you dinner on a tray, Mara."

She turned, looking a little wistful at the prospect. "Don't we have a dinner at the Severns'?"

"I'll send your excuses. Go have your

bath." He shoved her inside her door and firmly closed it.

She snuggled down in her warmed bed a little while later and sent the dinner tray away, food untasted. She was ill and feverish for more than a week, alternately shaken by chills when no amount of blankets seemed to warm her or so burningly hot she felt on fire and kicked her coverings loose.

The doctor came every day to pour soothing paregorics down her throat; her maid and the housekeeper nursed her in turn; flowers were delivered daily and the duke visited her bedside twice a day.

Only Roy stayed away . . . but in the black of evening when dreams and nightmares were strangely intermixed, she cried out for Duggie and Duggie seemed to come to her. He held her in his arms and stroked her flowing mane of hair. He comforted and consoled her.

When she was well and there were no more nightmares, Duggie went away too. It was a strangely empty feeling, like losing him again.

Presently her doctor announced her well enough to be carried downstairs to the morning parlor overlooking the gardens. She would sit on the lounge every day and weep in sorrow and self-pity and weakness.

The slightest thing set her off. Flowers from a friend. A loving note from Emma. A badly knit shawl from a seventeen-year-old girl who would probably be the first mother in her house.

"It's so ugly," she sobbed to Roy, who had taken the package from a footman and brought it to her. She spread the shawl across her knees. "And I look so terrible in brown."

"You don't have to wear it, you know," he suggested, a look of comical concern on his face.

"Her feelings would be hurt."

"I promise not to tell her," Roy pledged solemnly as he whisked the shawl off her knees and replaced it with a package of his own. "Here's something that should make your day brighter—a publisher's copy of Miss Austen's last work, *Persuasion*. I know how you love her books."

"Oh, Roy, thank you." She lifted her eager face to his, then commenced turning the unbound pages of the first volume. "I was so looking forward to this."

"Enjoy your reading day. I ordered the leather-bound edition for you when it comes out."

"How thoughtful. . . ." But she murmured it absently, her attention already caught by the first sentence.

Sir Walter Elliot, of Kellynch Hall, in Somersetshire, was a man who, for his own amusement, never took up any book but the Baronetage. . . .

When Roy and the duke returned from the

House in midafternoon, she had fallen asleep on the lounge, wrapped in the ugly wool shawl. The second volume of *Persuasion* lay open next to her outstretched hand.

Roy touched her cheeks with feather-light fingertips. "Wet. She's been crying again," he said softly.

"All over the book, too," his father observed, carefully lifting it. "Dear me."

"What?"

"This passage she appears to have underlined."

Roy looked over the duke's shoulder. They read together silently. The duke reined in his amusement as he saw his son's expression change from tenderness to indignation and then to anger.

Roy seemed to be struggling for breath. "She is saying . . . she presumes to think . . . Damnation, how dare she believe . . . ?"

Furiously, he read the offending lines again, this time out loud. *"All the privilege I claim for my own sex (it is not a very enviable one: you need not covet it), is that of loving longest, when existence or when hope is gone!"*

Mara blinked open her eyes to see two faces peering down at her, the duke's wryly amused, her husband's so irate, she blinked again in surprise and shock.

"You blind, blockish, self-maintained martyr! How dare you underline those words?" Roy's voice was choked with the same fury she saw on his face. He flung the book down on the lounge and limped rapidly out of the room.

Mara, wide awake now, looked up at her father-in-law. Unconsciously, she stroked her left cheek.

"The last time he looked at me like that," she mentioned matter-of-factly, "my face ached for a full day."

"I cannot begin to offer apologies for my son's conduct," the duke said slowly. "For Raleigh to strike you was inexcusable, but—"

Mara hunched an indifferent shoulder as she interrupted him. "I assure you that the slap, which I could have returned with interest had I cared to, was much more forgivable than the words he spoke."

"Again, I can't excuse him," the duke's soft, persuasive voice continued, "but have you ever considered that there was, if not provocation, at least great reason for his *un*reason? During the thirty hours or more before your quarrel he had been continuously in the saddle, part of that time in the thick of the terrible fighting at Quatre Bas, with the prospect of fiercer fighting ahead. His only food all day had been a stale roll, a half-raw chicken leg, and some wine. He had suffered cuts, bruises, and at least one bad fall when his horse was shot beneath him. He had seen his friends maimed and killed and sent other men he knew well to their deaths. He was stupid and dazed with hunger, fatigue, grief, and shock. Sent on an errand near to Brussels in the black of night and the deluge of rain and the middle of war's madness, he had been unable to resist going miles and hours out of his way for the chance of just a few short moments with you. He knew—none better—they might be your last."

Mara had covered both cheeks now and was crying into her hands.

"He reacted instinctively . . . abominably, no doubt, but he had loved you for so many years and for that same number been torn by jealousy mixed with shame at his feelings for the friend that he loved, too. To find the two of you in bed. . . . True, he acted irrationally, but was there not time for *you*," the father asked most pointedly, "to have run after *him* . . . for you to have reached him in time before he mounted and rode away? You might have called him every evil name you could lay your tongue to and yet conveyed the important message that needed to be given. *You rotten bastard, the only evil that exists is in your mind. This man is wounded, perhaps dying. I was offering him the warmth and comfort I would give to anyone in such a state, let alone a brother dearly loved.*"

Mara wiped her face with a flowing chiffon sleeve, and the duke paused to offer her an exquisitely folded linen handkerchief from his coat pocket. As she blew her nose vigorously, the remorseless voice continued.

"You chose—deliberately—to let him leave with that message unsaid. Forgive me . . . I know you suffered greatly yourself when your Duggie died . . . but I think you cannot shirk all responsibility for the unhappiness of these last years."

He passed a hand rather distractedly through his hair. "I should be the last one to reproach you. God knows I am haunted by my own failures as a father . . . which is, perhaps, why now, when he is the son most closely connected to my life and my interests, the son of my heart, I am . . . unmanned by his pain and grief. I had hoped that *you* would make up to him for all. Unfair of me, perhaps. It is certainly your right to put your own life first. I am only disappointed that your pride also takes first place over love."

Mara leaped up from her lounge with surprising energy. "That isn't fair!" she accused, flushed of cheeks but bright of eyes again.

"Isn't it?"

"He never even came to visit me all the while I was ill."

The duke could not help smiling a little at this seemingly irrelevant accusation.

"What did you expect," he asked gently, "after you had made such a point of a separate apartment and he had promised to respect your privacy? Not that he did, of course."

"He . . . he didn't?" Mara faltered.

"You were out of your head for several days during your sickness, tormented by terrible nightmares. So long as you were, Roy sat with you every night . . . took the place of your maid to nurse you . . . went into your bed to hold and comfort you when you cried out for Duggie. In other words, he was once again assuming the all-too-familiar role of being second to him."

"That isn't true!" Mara cried out impulsively. "Duggie was—well, he was Duggie, but Roy—I've been in love with Roy since the time—"

She turned away, blushing and biting at her lip.

"Since the night on the mountain?"

Her mouth quivered, but she faced him bravely. "Ever since that night," she affirmed.

"Why didn't you tell him?"

"Because he made it plain that he felt *obligated* to protect me." She flung up her head. "I was not going to be *noblesse oblige* for the duke's son."

"A pity you never asked the duke's son how *he* felt," sighed the duke, "and that *I* had given him so little esteem for himself, he was too fearful ever to tell you."

Then he clasped her hands warmly in both

of his. "I think, my dear, our concern is no longer so much the sorry past as it is whether you have sufficient courage to deal boldly with the future. Do you?"

Mara slapped the damped, balled-up handkerchief back into her father-in-law's reluctant hand.

"I do." It was like her wedding vow. "I do indeed."

Chapter Twenty-nine

She tripped over her unsteady feet twice on the way upstairs and leaned so heavily on Roy's door as she started to knock that it flew open of its own volition and she stumbled inside.

Roy sat in a chair, his valet kneeling to help him with his boots. Both men looked up, startled.

The valet's astonishment and Roy's blankly unwelcoming look almost undid her. About to flee the room again, Mara remembered the duke's question about courage. She gulped and displayed some. "Go away, please, Henry."

The valet looked helplessly toward Roy.

"Now!" said Mara.

Roy's lips twitched slightly. "You heard your mistress, Henry," he said, and the valet nodded, rose to his feet, and slipped out noiselessly.

Mara knelt in his place the better to look up at her husband.

"Why didn't you divorce me?" she asked.

"Why should I do anything so damn stupid when the most I've asked of life is to have you for my wife? And don't," he warned her, "tell me what I said in Brussels when I was out of my mind with pain and jealousy and . . . well, never mind."

Mara bowed her head a moment, waiting for her eyes to clear.

"Anyhow," his voice continued, almost sullen now, "even if I *had* gotten a divorce for the Brussels marriage, you would still have been my wife."

She looked up at him, her eyes tearless but puzzled. "I—don't understand."

"We've been married since that day at Gretna Green."

"I don't understand," she said again, very pale.

"We were married at Gretna, remember?"

"I remember, but—"

"There are no buts. I never got the first one annulled. I never even told my father about it until years later after I got back from Waterloo."

"But you wrote to me and said—"

"I said things were satisfactorily settled. Well, so they were—to my mind. The marriage stood. Only one other person besides those who were there in Scotland knew of it . . . Emma."

"Mam!"

"Yes, Mam. I told her everything before I left. The marriage was my safeguard so that in the years of separation I would know you were mine. Telling Mam was my safeguard so that if someone else came along . . . no, God damn it! that's not true. I've got to be honest; it was Duggie I was thinking of . . . I just wanted Mam to know you weren't marriageable."

"And if I had fallen in love with someone else?"

"In that case, provided there wasn't a child, I promised Mam I would arrange an annulment. I wasn't so selfish as to intend to keep you against your wishes."

"Why did you never say you loved me?"

"I did."

"I mean—before Brussels."

"Oh, for Christ's sakes, Mara, there are other ways of declaring love than with words. You were such a kid . . ."

"Such a kid that I made love with you gladly, willingly . . . no, eagerly on that mountain when I was just fourteen. I gave you what you called a precious gift . . . and all the years after while *you* cavorted on the Peninsula with señoritas and camp followers, getting your damned experience, I was waiting, remember? I was *needing,* too . . . I was . . . oh, hell!"

She began to cry quietly into the crook of one arm. "I know I shouldn't have gone off to

America," she sobbed. "I should have stayed and fought it out with you like—like a soldier! But I was hurting *so* over Duggie, I couldn't think right or act sensibly. I only . . . why didn't you come after me if you cared?"

"Help me off with my boot, please, Mara."

She lifted her tear-drenched face in puzzlement.

"Please."

The boot came off, not without a struggle, and Mara stayed crouched at his feet, the stuffed boot in her hand, her eyes fastened in sick dismay on the stump of his foot in the neatly folded-back silk stocking.

"A foot," said Roy's calm voice, "was not much to leave at Waterloo, compared to what so many men gave up there, but still—it hampered me. I was ill for a long time, and then came learning to walk again . . . and so much time to think about how I had mishandled you . . . our life . . . everything. I thought of going to America. God knows I wanted to, but I felt as though *I* deserved the penance of separation and *you* needed the time to come to terms with your grief."

Mara sat back on her heels, striving to be calm. "How noble of you! Do you realize that I thought I was divorced?" she asked, her indignation mounting. "I felt free to—Do you know that I received *five* proposals of marriage in America? Were you so sure of me? Or merely indifferent to whether I made a bigamous marriage?"

He eyed her warily. "As soon as I found out from Emma where you had gone, I wrote to Quincey apprising him of our situation. There was never any danger of a marriage."

"Oh, wasn't there?" said Mara ominously. "Why, you arrogant, overbearing son of a . . . duke, you."

He leaned over and plucked her off the floor and onto his lap. "Hush!" he said sternly. "For once in your life, just listen. I have been in love with you, perverted creature that I am, since you were hardly more than a child. We've been married for more than seven years, separated more than we've ever been together, and I can count on my fingers and toes—the ones I used to have included—the times in those years that we've ever made love. You have given me more grief, more pain, more tears—don't look at me like that; yes, I said tears . . . but also"—he grasped her mane of hair and pressed it against his lips—"also more joy than all the people in my life put together." He shook her slightly. "So you think women love longest when there is no hope. Never dare say such a thing again. Not to me."

"No, my lord."

"What do you mean, no, my lord?"

"I mean, I won't say it, my lord, if you don't want me to, even if . . ."

"Even if what?"

"Even if I believe it," whispered Mara. "You see, maybe I didn't always know it, but

I think I've loved you as long as you've loved me."

They sat staring at each other, eye to eye, till Roy said hoarsely, "What the hell are we waiting for?"

"I don't know, my lord Raleigh," said Mara in tones of sweet saintliness. "I thought, perhaps, working so close to the House of Lords, you'd become a man of . . . words . . . rather than deeds."

"You thought what?" roared Roy in righteous indignation, tumbling her off his lap and back onto the floor, where she lay, sprawled, looking up at him and laughing. "I'll give you words." He wrenched off his other boot and reached for the cane. "Take off your dressing gown and get into that bed, you hussy. I'll show you deeds."

"Lock the door," said Mara, still laughing as she walked to the bed and slowly began to strip. "I should hate for us to be interrupted."

"Nothing—no one—would venture to interrupt us until tomorrow," Lord Raleigh Irwine told her firmly.

Nothing . . . and no one . . . did.

Jude Deveraux

*America's favorite historical
romance author!*

THE JAMES RIVER TRILOGY

_____ Counterfeit Lady 43560/$3.95

_____ Lost Lady 43556/$3.95

_____ River Lady 45405/$3.95

And enter the passionate world of the
CHANDLER TWINS

_____ Twin of Ice 50049/$3.95

_____ Twin of Fire 50050/$3.95

POCKET BOOKS, Department JRT
1230 Avenue of the Americas, New York, N.Y. 10020

Please send me the books I have checked above. I am enclosing $_____ (please
add 75¢ to cover postage and handling for each order. N.Y.S. and N.Y.C. residents
please add appropriate sales tax). Send check or money order—no cash or C.O.D.'s
please. Allow up to six weeks for delivery. For purchases over $10.00, you may use
VISA: card number, expiration date and customer signature must be included.

NAME _____

ADDRESS _____

CITY _____ STATE/ZIP _____

729

Japestry

HISTORICAL ROMANCES

POCKET BOOKS.